DAYDREAMER

As Brad walked down the sideline of the football field, his eyes met mine for a moment. Then his face lit with a smile as he leaned over to say to me, "You want to come to a party tomorrow night? I'll pick you up at eight, OK?"

"OK," I managed to say.

"Great," he said and ran off.

"Now I know why you look so good tonight," Shannon said knowingly. "Brad Sorenson!" She looked impressed.

All I could do was grin. I almost needed to pinch myself to see if this was real, or another of my famous daydreams. It had happened just like I had imagined it would, I realized in wonder.

Daydreamer

Janet Quin-Harkin

BANTAM BOOKS
TORONTO · NEW YORK · LONDON · SYDNEY

RL 6, IL age 11 and up

DAYDREAMER

A Bantam Book / February 1983

ISBN 0-553-23190-1

Published simultaneously in the United States and Canada

Bantam Books are published by Bantam Books, Inc. Its trademark,
consisting of the words "Bantam Books" and the portrayal of a
rooster, is Registered in U.S. Patent and Trademark Office and in
other countries. Marca Registrada. Bantam Books, Inc., 666 Fifth
Avenue, New York, New York 10103.

PRINTED IN THE UNITED STATES OF AMERICA

O   0 9 8 7 6 5 4 3 2 1

Daydreamer

Chapter One

I relaxed in my first-class seat, sipping a Coke and looking around me. My clogs lay at my feet where I had kicked them off. I squirmed in my seat, wishing my Gloria Vanderbilt jeans weren't quite so snug. Below me the parched brown landscape of Southern California gave way to the rich farmlands of the central valley, thousands of little squares of green divided by neat, straight lines.

As I tossed my long blond hair back, I heard a whisper behind me. "Doesn't that girl look like Lana Daniels?"

"Lana Daniels, the movie star?"

"Yeah. She looks just like her—same coloring, same hair. I wonder if she's her daughter or something."

"She could be. A kid traveling on her own in first class has got to be somebody. Maybe she's going to visit her mother. Imagine living in Hollywood, visiting movie sets . . ."

I couldn't help smiling. Their comments were so accurate. I *was* longing to see my mother again. I could picture her standing by the gate at the airport, looking cool and lovely as she always did, a mink draped casually around her shoulders, not even noticing the admiring glances or the whispers around her. Then, as she caught sight of me, she would throw aside her cool pose. "My baby!" she would yell, loud enough for the whole airport to hear. "Come and let me hug you." And I wouldn't even care that the whole airport was watching. . . .

"Miss, hey, miss!" Someone was shaking my shoulder roughly. I opened my eyes to find myself staring into a strange, wrinkled face wearing a peaked cap. I must have jumped a mile. He smiled at me.

"Sorry I startled you, miss, but didn't you say you was going to Sonoma? Well, we're here. This is where the bus stops."

I looked around me, confused. There were lots of people staring at me, just as there had been in my airport fantasy. Only this time I *did* mind their staring. Once more my daydreaming had made me look like a fool. I dragged myself back to reality. I wasn't on a plane, of course. I was at the back of a Greyhound bus, and I was not going to visit my mother. I was going to live with my grandmother, whom I hardly knew.

Red-faced and feeling stupid, I got up and fumbled with my suitcase, which was wedged into the luggage rack. I staggered down the aisle with it while all those faces watched me, showing no emotion at all.

Then I was outside, standing under a row of tall palm trees in the middle of a square. All

round it were old buildings, like something
out of a movie set. Huge old trees—cedars and
pines and palms—cast pools of deep shade.
Ducks splashed busily in a little pond. It all
seemed very warm and comfortable, especially
when I noticed the families sitting together on
the grass—the old people talking while the
little kids toddled around them. One little boy
ran toward me, fell down, and started crying.
Immediately a pretty young woman rushed to
scoop him up and comfort him.

Then I remembered why I was there. I began
to feel that awful panic I sometimes feel when I
am traveling on my own. What if my grandmother didn't show up to meet me? How could
I find her house? Did I have enough money to
pay for a taxi? What arrangements had my father actually made with her during those last,
painful phone calls?

Someone tapped me on the arm, and I
turned to find myself looking into a kind, ques-
tioning face. I wondered how I hadn't recognized her before. She was an older, rounder
version of Dad, with the same peaked hairline
and the same little dimple in the middle of her
chin.

"Lisa?" she said hesitantly.

"Grandma?"

We stood looking at each other uncertainly,
then we gave each other a big hug. I was glad to
feel strong arms, like those of my father, around
me. At least she wasn't going to be the frail

little old lady I had pictured and feared.

"I'd never have recognized you," she said. "The last time I saw you, you were only about ten or eleven. You had braces on your teeth, and your hair was quite blond."

"I used to swim all the time in those days," I said. "My hair was more chlorine green than blond!"

"Well, I was standing here looking for a blond like your mother," Grandma said, smiling. "Now that I look at you, I think you're actually much more like Jack. You have his dark eyes and long lashes, and, I guess, if you'd come from a less sunny climate, your hair would be dark, too. But I think it's pretty just the way it is. I'd call it—honey blond. Goodness, you're petite, Lisa," she went on.

I couldn't think of an answer to that, so I just stood there, watching a line of ants drag a leaf of rye grass over the dusty ground.

Then my grandmother stopped examining me and grabbed my suitcase. "Well, let's not stand around here all day. After that bus ride, I know you'd like a nice soak in a tub and something cool to drink."

She set off at a brisk trot ahead of me.

"Here, I'll carry that," I said, trying to catch up with her and take the suitcase.

She only smiled and walked faster. "Nonsense, child, I'm used to hard work. Your grandpa's been dead for fifteen years, and I've run the place alone since then, with no help from anyone."

She said it proudly, and I felt proud of her, too, but I felt a twinge of guilt. I also felt angry at my parents. She had been only a day's drive away from us all these years. Why hadn't we helped her? I could have come up to her over vacations to make things easier for her. But I knew she and my mother didn't get along. I clearly remembered my mother saying, "I won't have that old dragon here telling me I'm a sloppy housekeeper." Then my mother hadn't been around for a while, and my father had never known what to do with me over the long vacations. Surely helping Grandma would have been preferable to all those boring and expensive summer camps they shipped me off to each June.

We crossed the square, walking from sunlight to dappled shade. My grandmother stopped beside an ancient Cadillac with fins and lots of chrome. There was a box of tomatoes on the backseat, which gave the whole car a sharp smell. She pushed them over to make room for my suitcase.

We drove along at a leisurely pace, the street bordered by white fences and blooming flowers. It was a long time since I had driven slowly enough to take a good look at the things I passed. My father always drove his Porsche as if he were trying out for the Indy 500, and I was always so busy hanging on that I never looked out of the window. I bet his mother's driving used to make him mad, I thought. My father wasn't exactly known for his calm temperament.

I shut him out of my mind with an effort of will and studied the scenery. The white-painted houses with their sun porches seemed to have come straight out of a thirties movie. They looked like they belonged in the classic Hollywood version of a sleepy country town where a boy and girl might fall in love over malteds at the sweet shop, get married in a little white church, and live happily ever after. Would that ever happen to me? At that moment, I badly needed someone to love me.

I glanced across at my grandmother, her eyes narrowed against the glare of the sun as she concentrated on her driving. Had she really wanted me to come here, or had she taken me only because I had no place else to go? I wished I could have overheard what was said on her end of that telephone conversation when my father explained about his daughter needing a woman's influence—and his needing to follow his career.

As we drove out of town, the small, neat yards gave way to bigger spreads with ranch houses hidden behind eucalyptus trees.

"Well, this is it," said my grandmother. "Not too far from town, but a bit too far to walk. We'll find you a bicycle."

She swung the car onto a gravel drive. Oleander bushes almost as big as trees, each a mass of pink or white flowers, shielded the house from the street. A rickety sign saying Fresh Eggs was tacked to the gatepost. The front lawn was brown and dusty, and the house looked tired and saggy but somehow peaceful. It was two stories and painted white, with a balcony along the front making a shady porch below it. It must have been quite elegant once, but now it was run-down. The white paint was peeling, and the massive grapevine climbing up one side of the porch threatened to bring the whole thing down.

We climbed out of the car, and I stood listening to the silence. In our Hollywood apartment there had never been silence. Usually the air conditioner was humming. If the window was open, the noise of the traffic drifted in, even in the middle of the night. And there were always planes overhead. Here the only sounds were a cicada screeching in the bushes and a bee buzzing among hibiscus flowers.

"How do you like it?" Grandma asked.

"It's so peaceful," I said.

She gave me a sideways look. "Yes, well, you may find it a little too peaceful after the sort of life you've been used to. We don't go in for parties here. And I hope you won't find it lonely."

I wanted to tell her no one could have been lonelier than the girl who let herself into an empty apartment every afternoon and cooked dinner for a father who often didn't show up to eat it until two in the morning. But instead I just smiled and made myself say, "I'm sure I'm going to like it here."

Although I was not sure at all.

Chapter Two

After my grandmother had dumped my suit-case on my bed, showed me how to open the closet door when it stuck, which drawers to put my clothes in, and how to kick the pipe behind the bathtub so the faucet would work, she hurried downstairs, leaving me alone. I heard her making efficient noises in the kitchen.

Well, one thing was sure: she was not at all like the grandmother I had imagined. I had pictured a little, old, white-haired lady sitting on the porch rocking while she knitted. I had a feeling this grandmother never sat and rocked. From my hazy memories of her few visits, I had also gotten the impression she was a nervous person. Now it was quite clear she was not like that at all; she just must have felt out of place in our world. Perhaps she was also nervous about being with my mother. Lots of people were.

I took a good look around the room that was to be my home for the indefinite future. It was old-fashioned and would have made my mother shiver in horror, but I found it sort of comforting. It looked like a room that had al-ways been there, unchanged. The bed was incredibly high, and I pictured myself pole-vaulting into it. It was covered in a faded patchwork quilt. The rest of the furniture was big and heavy, with lots of curly bits at the corners. It looked as if it had been around even longer than my grandmother. My mother would have called it "early Salvation Army."

On the wall was a picture of a ship sailing in a rough sea. Three porcelain wild ducks were flying in formation across the other wall, and on the dresser were two silver cups. On one was inscribed, To John David Daniels. Outstanding Orator 1947; and on the other were the words, John Daniels. Daily Chronicle Creative Writing Cup 1949.

So he had found his vocation way back then! The future journalist and broadcaster had been recognized in his small hometown. I realized this must have been my father's old room, and I found that comforting, too.

I walked across to the window. It was half-open and the white, frilly curtain stirred in the late afternoon breeze. Below me were rows of tomatoes and other growing things that I, being a city girl, didn't recognize. There were fruit trees beyond—I thought they were peach and apple trees, but I wasn't sure. I decided I would have to study up on horticulture quickly! I definitely recognized the lemon tree in the corner, however, because we had one of those on our own patio in Hollywood. To the left of the garden was a high wire fence, which I guessed was a chicken coop, since there had been a sign outside advertising eggs. Beyond the chicken coop, I could see part of the neighboring house. In the distance was nothing but hill after hill of vineyards disappearing to where they rose steeply to form the boundary of the Valley of the Moon. At this time of day, the whole scene was bathed in a warm, rosy light and was so beautiful it nearly took my breath away.

"I will like it here. I know I will," I told myself. "Who could be unhappy with a view like that?"

Suddenly something touched the back of my legs. A gentle, velvet caress, which was completely unexpected. I let out a huge scream and spun around just in time to see a cat shoot away, then plop itself down to stare at me, at a safe distance, in offended silence.

My grandmother came running up the stairs. "What's wrong, Lisa?" she called. "Did I hear you scream?"

"It's OK, Grandma. The cat rubbed against my leg and scared me, that's all."

My grandmother laughed. "That's only Jellybean. He was just trying to be friendly and say hello."

"I'm sorry to bring you upstairs for nothing," I said, feeling foolish. "But I'm just not used to cats. And he sort of snuck up on me. . . . Why is he called Jellybean? That's a funny name for a cat."

"That's just what I said when your father called the first one Jellybean. He was only about seven years old at the time. He brought home a stray kitten he had found, and he begged to keep it, so finally we let him. 'Jellybean is a strange name for a cat,' I said to him, and do you know what he said? He said, 'Well, I love jellybeans, and I love this cat; so when I think of jellybeans they will remind me of him, and when I think of him, he will remind me of jellybeans.' "

I laughed. "Just the sort of thing my father would say."

"So I've called all my cats Jellybean ever since—to remind me of the boy I used to have," Grandma said wistfully.

Suddenly I felt very close to her. I saw her as I was—hurt and alone, abandoned by the people she wanted to love best. But we were still strangers to each other, so I couldn't find the right words to tell her I understood. Instead I said brightly, "It will be nice to have a cat around the house. Mama was allergic to animal hair, so we never had any pets."

"Well, you can take over my twenty-five chickens for me," Grandma said. "They'll be pets enough for anyone!"

She was chuckling as she walked back down the stairs, sounding somewhat like an old chicken herself.

Later, after I took a bath and changed my clothes, we sat in her large kitchen and ate together. The kitchen was cool, even on a hot summer night like that one. The stove was in a little, separate room so that it didn't make the house too hot.

"I had that built myself," my grandmother said. "I got the idea from the early settlers. They always had a separate kitchen. I can never understand why other folks don't do the same."

At one end of the kitchen was a big, white cabinet full of decorative plates; otherwise, it was a pretty functional sort of room. Not like my kitchen at home, which my mother had decorated before she moved out. It was so full of houseplants that tendrils draped themselves over your food while you tried to eat, and it had walls covered with copper pots nobody ever cooked in.

We ate in silence. Grandma had fixed a platter of cold ham and lots of homegrown salad.

"I thought cold would be best for tonight," she said. "I wasn't sure whether you'd be here on time. Besides, I think cold goes down better on hot summer evenings like this one."

I nodded. I was hungry, and busy eating everything in sight.

"Well, Lisa," Grandma said, "you're not at all how I'd thought you'd be. For one thing, look at you eat! I thought Hollywood people were always on some crazy diet."

"Not me," I said. "I like food too much. Besides, it doesn't seem to make much difference how much I eat. I don't get fat. Mama was always jealous of that. She has to watch her weight all the time."

"You take after your father," my grandmother said. "He always burned it off. Never stood still for a moment."

She played halfheartedly with a lone lettuce leaf on her plate. Then she said lightly, "So your father's off on an adventure, is he?"

"It's a great assignment. Middle East correspondent for NBC," I said, trying to keep my voice even.

"Too good to turn down and too risky to take his daughter. That's what he told me."

"That's what he told me, too. He thought I'd be in too much danger out there. Besides, I didn't really want to go." I didn't add that what I really wanted was a nice, secure family like everyone else had, with a mother and a father who came home every night and took care of me.

Grandma sniffed. "And your mother? What's she doing with herself now?"

I shrugged casually. "I wouldn't know. I haven't seen her in over a year."

"Not seen her in over a year? What kind of mother is that?"

"A mother whose career is important to her, I guess," I said, feeling I ought to defend her at least a little. After all, she *was* my mother.

"What career can be more important than bringing up your children properly?" my grandmother demanded fiercely.

Don't ask me, I thought. I agree with you. But try to get my parents to believe that.

Chapter Three

Grandma lived up to her word about the chickens. Early the next morning she informed me they were all mine, gave me a pail of chicken feed, and sent me out to give it to them.

"Just scatter it around," she said. "That's all there is to it."

I walked down the yard between the rows of tomatoes and let myself into the wire enclosure, wishing very much that my first pet could have been something more cuddly and less flighty than a swarm of hungry chickens. When the chickens saw a stranger approaching, they squawked and fluttered to the other side of the pen. Then, when they had recovered from their first fright, the smartest one noticed her regular food pail being held in the stranger's hand. She gave an excited squawk and dashed toward me. The others followed. Gingerly I scattered a small handful of corn in front of them. They fell upon it as if they had been starving for weeks.

In a flash I was surrounded by chickens— millions of squawking, clucking, pecking chickens all trying to get at my pail at once. They were climbing on my feet, pecking at my legs, fluttering up, and trying to land on my arms.

"Shoo," I yelled. "Get off. Go away." How does a person discipline chickens?

I tried to shake out the rest of the chicken food, but I couldn't. The solid mass of chickens had practically immobilized me. At that moment I remembered Alfred Hitchcock's movie, *The Birds.* I wondered how much of it was based on truth. Oh, well, maybe I would make medical history—maybe even the *Guinness Book of World Records.* I even wrote a hasty movie script as I tried to back away.

KILLER CHICKENS . . . THEY TEAR A YOUNG GIRL TO PIECES, THEN TERRORIZE A WHOLE TOWN!

My movie script was cut short as I stepped backward into their water dish, lost my balance, and fell over. Suddenly the chickens were not just on my feet, they were all over me. I did the only thing I could do—I screamed. At that moment it seemed that this was the worst thing that had ever happened to me.

"You got a problem?" A voice spoke from above me. It didn't sound like my grandmother's voice. God, perhaps? I peered up through the feathers and beaks. There was a boy's face looking down from the next yard. The wide face of a sunny country boy with freckles and sandy hair and very blue eyes.

"No, I'm fine," I called back as I struggled to

my feet. "No problem. Just getting to know these chickens a little better."

The boy grinned. "They might be less—less friendly if you weren't covered with their food," he said.

I saw what he meant. I was coated with chicken feed. I also had a wet seat from sitting in the chicken water. I jumped up and brushed myself off as quickly as I could. Immediately the chickens turned their attention from me to the cascade of food, and I stepped safely out of the way.

"That was close," I said. "I thought I was a goner."

The boy laughed. "I don't think there is a single documented case of death by chickens," he said. "Why didn't you just scatter the food and go?"

"Because I've never done this before!" I snapped. Now that I was back on my feet, I was beginning to feel suitably embarrassed. "Furthermore, until today I've never even seen a chicken! Except frozen in the supermarket. And frankly, I like them better that way."

The boy laughed again. "Well, if it's not a rude question, what on earth made you take a job like this?"

"A job like this?"

"Aren't you Mrs. Daniels's hired help?"

I looked at him with as much dignity as I could muster—which wasn't much, what with the feathers and my wet seat—and said, "I am not Mrs. Daniels's hired help. I am Mrs. Daniels's granddaughter."

"No kidding?" he said, not laughing any more. "We never knew she had any relatives. Nobody ever came to visit her. Where were you all these years?"

All things considered, I felt this question was unfair. Also impolite. Suddenly I wanted to get away. I knew I looked a mess, and I resented his questions. "We were in Hollywood," I said in my most Hollywood-type voice. "My mother's an actress, and we never had time for trips to little hick towns." I turned on my heel and stalked off.

Afterward, when I had shaken out the chicken feathers and taken a long hot shower, I felt very foolish. Every time I replayed that embarrassing scene in my mind, I felt like blushing scarlet.

If you behave like that, Lisa Daniels, I said to myself, you are not going to make too many friends around here.

I remembered I had promised myself I'd never mention that my mother was an actress. Outside of Hollywood that would be a disadvantage. Besides, the kids would want to know what movies she had been in lately, and then I'd have to tell them that she hadn't made a movie in several years and her greatest hit was *Bride of the Mummy* way back in the sixties. I didn't even like to remind *myself* of the cold, hard facts. It made me feel better if I pretended ner career was at least worth deserting us for. I preferred to think of my mother as the star, the beautiful blond with the mink around her shoulders, going from one successful movie to the next.

As I pulled on my khaki shorts and my white T-shirt, I thought about that boy again—how he had made fun of me, his laugh, his annoying questions. I imagined how he would look if my mother actually did decide to visit me. He would be working in his yard, dressed in his farm overalls, as the white Mercedes drew up. Mama would step out, dressed in a simple white silk dress, a subtle mink stole, and some understated diamond jewelry. Her long blond curls would be cascading over her shoulders.

"Young man," she would call in her low musical voice.

He would come over to her, stunned by her beauty, amazed at her elegance.

"Young man, I'm looking for the Daniels residence," she would say.

"It's right next door, ma'am," he would mumble. He would practically be speechless.

"Why, thank you," she would say, flashing her famous smile. "I've come to visit my daughter, who is staying there."

"But aren't you Lana Daniels, the movie star?" he would stutter.

"Of course," she would say, sweeping past him.

Then it would be all around school in a

matter of hours that Lana Daniels, well-known movie star, had come all the way to Sonoma just to visit her daughter Lisa. . . .

Well, that probably wouldn't happen—not quite that way. But I knew one thing. Somehow I would redeem myself in the eyes of that boy. He'd never see me making a fool of myself again. I wondered if we would go to the same school and if he was the type of person who'd never forget an incident like that. Perhaps it would be best to steer clear of him for a while.

Chapter Four

"Lisa, can you come down here for a minute, please?" I heard my grandmother calling. I was lying on my bed feeling hot and sleepy. At home I was used to a dip in the pool when the weather got too hot. Not only did this house have no pool, it wasn't even air-conditioned. And by late afternoon my bedroom was like an oven. Now I was lying down deciding whether I had the energy to take another shower.

One problem was that I wasn't used to all the chores. Of course I helped around the house at home, loading the dishwasher and keeping my room clean, as well as cooking. Cooking, however, really meant taking something out of the freezer and putting it in a preheated oven. But here I had real chores, honest-to-goodness pioneer chores. With my grandmother I had watered acres of plants with a hose, which seemed to have a mind of its own and couldn't pass a single rock or twig without becoming caught up in it. I had picked peppers and zucchini; I had helped to cut up the zucchini to freeze; and I had helped make zucchini bread. If this was what my grandmother described as

21

a "nice, quiet day to get you all settled in," I was dreading the busy ones.

"Coming!" I called, getting up and grabbing an old cotton housecoat that was hanging on the back of the bedroom door.

I wonder what we're going to do now, I thought as I reached the landing. Maybe just butcher a small hog or put up a few hundred jars of jam or something.

I trailed down the stairs and into the kitchen. "Where are you?" I called into the empty room.

"In here, in the sitting room," came Grandma's voice.

The sitting room was the big, cool room at the front of the house. It was full of heavy, old furniture, hangings, ornaments, and photographs—all Grandma's treasures. It was sort of like walking into a museum.

I pushed the door open. My grandmother was sitting on the faded velvet sofa, the one that used to be red but now was various shades of pink and gray. She was pouring coffee from a silver coffee pot. In the two chairs facing her were two other people, a pleasant-looking woman with sandy hair and a freckled face—and with her the boy from next door, the one I was going to impress soon.

I must have frozen in the doorway, only too aware of my horrible appearance. I hadn't even brushed my hair, and I was wearing a cotton robe patterned with hideous gigantic red and purple roses.

"Hi," the boy said cheerfully.

"Well, Lisa, isn't this nice?" my grandmother said.

I considered that. No, it wasn't really *nice*.

"These are our neighbors, the Gibsons. They just popped in to meet you. This is Mrs. Gibson and her son, Mike. You and Mike will go to the high school together."

"Hello," I said weakly.

"I'm pleased to meet you, Lisa," Mrs. Gibson said warmly. "It will be nice for Mike to have someone from school living so close by. He'll probably be calling you all the time for help with his homework."

Mike had the grace to blush. I managed a sort of smile. There was a pause during which we all listened to the clock ticking.

"Mike's a junior this year," Mrs. Gibson said.

"Lisa's going to be a junior, too, aren't you?" my grandmother said.

I continued to stand there like an idiot, wondering what spell I could mutter to make the floor open up and swallow me.

"Well, dear, sit down and have a cup of my good coffee," Grandma said.

"And if you want to come take a dip in our pool afterward," Mrs. Gibson said, "you're welcome to. Oh, it's just a Doughboy—nothing like your fancy Hollywood pools—but it sure cools you off on a day like this."

"Thanks," I said. "I could do with cooling off. I was about to take a shower when Grandma called me down." I paused. "I didn't realize anyone else was in the house, or I would have put some clothes on first." I thought I should try to explain that I didn't usually go around in a housecoat with purple roses on it.

"So you and Mike will be in the same grade at school," Grandma said again. "That will be so nice for you. You'll have someone to show you around."

"It'll probably seem like a small school after what you've been used to," Mrs. Gibson said. "Only seven hundred students from up and down the valley. But at least you get to know everybody, and that's nice. We have a really good football team, and everyone goes to the games on Friday nights. And there are lots of clubs. I bet you can find something to interest you."

"Yeah, how about future farmers?" Mike said, giving me a knowing smile. "You could do a project on chickens."

"What day does school start?" I asked Mrs. Gibson, pretending Mike didn't exist. I certainly wasn't going to have him telling the chicken story to my grandmother.

"The Wednesday after Labor Day. That's less than two weeks away," Mrs. Gibson replied. "Do you have your schedule yet?"

"No," I said. "I don't have anything. Coming to stay with my grandmother was sort of a last-minute decision. I was all set to go back to Hollywood High when my father got this job abroad."

Mrs. Gibson sighed. "Well, I guess a lot of kids today are used to moving around and changing schools. But here in the Valley of the Moon, we're old stick-in-the muds. We'd never want to move."

"Speak for yourself, Ma," Mike said. "I can't wait to get out into the big, wicked world." He grinned at me.

"Lisa is going to meet the principal tomorrow," Grandma said. "Then she'll be able to get her schedule straightened out and see the school."

"Lucky Lisa!" Mike said. "I hope you manage to stay awake. Mr. Schiffman could be packaged as a sleeping pill. He'll look at you over his glasses, and he'll say, 'Um, Miss—er—Daniels—I—er—can't tell you—er—what a pleasure it is—er—um—to welcome you to—er—this—um—school'!"

The next day when he really did say it, I had to bite my bottom lip to keep myself from laughing. After he finished welcoming me, which took at least half an hour and did very nearly put me in dreamland, he took me on a tour of the school. He escorted me personally! I couldn't believe it. At home the principal would have called a student or one of the office staff to do that sort of thing. I guessed smaller schools were good for the personal touch.

But I would rather have wandered around alone. It would have been much quicker, too, as he gave me a complete speech at each classroom door. And, in fact, I didn't really need a tour at all, since most of the high school was housed in one simple red brick building two stories high, and the classrooms were numbered in a logical order.

"I don't want to take up all your time, Mr. Schiffman," I said when it began to look as if the tour would take several hours. "I'm sure I can find my own way around, and you must be very busy."

"Oh, no, I'm delighted," he said. "More than delighted. I'm—er—very proud of my school, and I—er—love showing it off to people."

So I got the complete guided tour. I could see what Mike had said about his boring people to death.

"Now this, as you can see, is our science laboratory. We have—er—twenty-four Bunsen burners and two sinks. . . ."

"This—is where you will have math. Mr. Caufield teaches geometry, which, I believe, is the class to which you have been assigned."

I kept very quiet about the fact that I would have been in trigonometry, except I flunked geometry the year before. That was too embarrassing to admit, especially since the reason that I flunked was that I had a crush on my geometry teacher, Mr. Phillips. I started to think about him now, as Mr. Schiffman droned on. Randy Phillips. He was tall and great-looking. Not much older than his students, in fact, and when he smiled, he had dimples in his cheeks. I spent every math period just gazing at him, imagining what it would be like if suddenly he noticed me and saw how different I was from all the rest of his students.

The school year went by, and still he hadn't fallen madly in love with me. I kept finding really unusual problems to get help with after school, but it was no good. He was friendly and helpful, but I was just another student who somehow hadn't gotten the hang of external angles.

Then one day I had this really fantastic daydream of how the school caught fire and he was trapped upstairs and nobody would dare to climb up and rescue him—except me. I climbed that burning building and dragged him down, even though he weighed a hundred and eighty-five pounds, and I weigh only a hundred and ten. He was just about to bestow his eternal gratitude on me, in the form of a kiss, when I heard him calling my name. . . . He was asking me some dumb question about a pie.

"What sort of a pie?" I asked.

The class burst out laughing. He was talking about the mathematical pi, of course. He thought it was a great joke and teased me about it.

"By using pi, and for Lisa's information it is a blueberry pie, not a pumpkin pie. . . ." he said. I was the only one in the class who didn't laugh. . . .

I came back to consciousness to hear Mr. Schiffman saying, "So we can count on you to do that, can't we?"

"Oh, definitely," I answered, not knowing if I had promised to be a good student or to be the school janitor for the whole year. I made a quick mental note to pay attention the whole year and not get emotionally involved with any teachers, especially math teachers. I hoped Mr. Caufield would be old and fat.

After what seemed like hours, we finished touring the main building, then walked over to the gymnasium. Mr. Schiffman wanted to know what sports I was interested in. I didn't like to say none, so I mumbled something about volleyball. He was all set to sign me up for the girls' volleyball team right then. If he'd ever seen me play volleyball, he would have saved his breath.

Then we saw the music room, which was one of those prefabs set up in back of the school. (I always called them outhouses.) He asked me if I played an instrument. When I admitted I had had clarinet lessons, his face lit up. "Then you must join our school band," he said. "They play at all the football games. You'll enjoy it, and you'll meet a lot of students that way."

I didn't really care whether I met anybody. I

28

mean, of course, I wanted friends, but I was also afraid of making friends. In the end, it seemed you just lost them. I'd had "best" friends in elementary school. Then their parents would get divorced, or they'd move away or something, and I'd never see them again. When that happened once too often—about the same time my mother moved out—I vowed I would be nice to everyone but never get that close to a friend again. It wasn't worth getting hurt.

But I did think a bit about joining the marching band. It was crystal clear Mr. Schiffman was determined to get me involved in something, and the marching band didn't sound too bad. I had enjoyed my clarinet lessons, and it would be fun to play with other people and go to the games. And it would be a lot better than spending long evenings watering tomatoes and avoiding chickens. Who knew, if I didn't find my own amusement, Grandma really might sign me up for future farmers!

"OK," I said to Mr. Schiffman. "You can put me down for the marching band."

When I got back to Grandma's after the school tour, it was the middle of the day and deadly hot. Grandma was weeding the flower garden but stopped when she saw me. "Hi," she called. "How did it go?"

"OK," I said.

Grandma wiped her forehead with a hanky. I wished I had a hanky so I could do that, too. I was sticky and uncomfortable from the long walk home.

"How about some iced tea?" she asked, stepping over the little wire fence that supposedly protected the flowers from Jellybean.

"Oh, that sounds great," I said, then sighed. "I can't believe how hot it is."

I helped Grandma make a pitcher of iced tea, and we sat out on the porch with it. At first we were too busy cooling ourselves to talk, but finally Grandma asked what had happened at school.

"Well," I said, choosing my words carefully, "I think my classes are going to be good, but I'll have to work hard in math. I signed up for marching band."

"You did? That's terrific!"

It was? I wasn't used to such enthusiasm over my interests.

"The school's very—" I paused.

"Small?" supplied Grandma.

I grinned. "Well, yeah."

"That's OK. It's a small town. We accept these things. Are you worried about making friends, Lisa?" Grandma asked gently.

I stared into my drink. "I guess."

Grandma waited for me to go on.

"I'm afraid with so few kids, I'm really going to stick out as the new girl."

"Well, maybe you will for awhile. But you won't be the new girl forever. Besides, you know

Mike. He'll introduce you to his friends. I know he'll be glad to help you out."

Just what I need, I thought miserably. More of Mike's help.

"Lisa," said my grandmother, "I want you to know I'm on your side. I'm here to help you. I hope you'll come to me if you have any problems."

I smiled at her gratefully. "Thanks, Grandma," I said.

Chapter Five

The night before school started, I couldn't get to sleep. It was a very hot night. Although my window was wide open, the drapes did not stir. I lay on top of the sheet and tossed and turned. It seemed as if I would never be able to sleep.

"Will you just relax," I told myself firmly. "Now you're worrying because you can't sleep. Nobody was ever the worse for missing one night's sleep. Remember what Mama used to say—lie there and think beautiful thoughts."

But nothing helped, not beautiful thoughts or counting sheep. I tried counting beautiful sheep. No good. I lay there with eyes that prickled when I tried to close them and thought about school. What would it be like? Would the other kids accept me, or would I be an outsider? Would all the decent boys already be going steady, or would somebody be left over for me? A special boy just waiting for me to come along?

Then there was the question of clothes. What should I wear on my first day? That was very important. That afternoon I had gone through my wardrobe, a very depressing task. My clothes were all last year's, and they looked it. I didn't have one outfit that would make me look like Lisa Daniels, fresh out of Hollywood.

I knew I could never tell the kids at school the reason for my lack of clothes. How would they understand about my mother and her debts? Mama never had any idea about money. When she saw something she liked, she bought it. She had once been rich, and it was hard to break her old habits. So when she left us, she also left a mountain of debts my father was still trying to pay off.

If my mother was hopeless about money, my father was hopeless about clothes. He wore clothes only because the law doesn't allow people to run around naked. But he never cared what he was wearing. And he never could get it into his head that girls of my age needed new clothes from time to time.

"It still fits, doesn't it?" he'd said when I showed him one of last year's sweaters. So I was stuck with faded jeans that were a bit too short, T-shirts with inane messages printed on them, and sweaters with little fuzzy balls on them.

I had to get some new clothes, I decided. It was obvious my grandmother didn't have a whole lot of money. And I had no idea what arrangements my father had made with her about money for me. Grandma was pretty open with me about most things, but where my parents were concerned, I often felt her backing off. And she had said before, she was on my side and wanted to help me. She felt my parents had wronged me, had been unfair to me. She wanted to try to make up for all that unfairness herself and practically pretended my parents didn't exist. But she didn't realize that one way to help me would be to talk about my parents. I needed to. I couldn't give up on them. They were too much a part of me.

Anyway, to get back to the clothes, whenever I tried to get some sort of dim idea of what she and Dad had talked about before I left Hollywood, Grandma would set her mouth in a stubborn line.

We were sitting in the kitchen surrounded by jars and paraffin and sugar and raspberries the day before school began. Grandma was trying to teach me the fine art of preserving, and I was actually enjoying myself, but needless to say my mind wandered from time to time. I had just finished a disturbing daydream in which I had had to go to school the first day dressed in two potato sacks and a feedbag. So I was broaching the subject of my wardrobe with Grandma.

"Grandma?" I asked. "Did you talk to Dad before he left?"

"Yes," she answered. That was when she set her mouth in a line.

I tried a different approach. "You know my clothes, Grandma?"

"Not personally," she said, the line disappearing.

I laughed. "They're on the old side."

"Would you like some new ones for school?"

"Yes," I said, "but I don't have much money."

"Well," said Grandma, "we'll figure something out. I have a little money."

It turned out she had seventy-eight dollars in her "mad money" jar, which I was not about to touch. It was *her* fun money, not mine. That was when I figured she probably wasn't getting much money from Mom or Dad, at least not enough for a bunch of new clothes. I thought about it awhile and finally reached a decision. I'd better get a job, I thought, as soon as I've settled into school.

At the thought of school the next day, I could feel my stomach beginning to churn. If it will all just go OK, I thought. Just OK. I'm not asking for terrific or even good. Just don't let anyone laugh at me, and don't let me daydream and do something stupid. All I want is OK.

I knew I should try to sleep, but I found myself tuning in to the movie theater in my head. There I was in my new outfit—designer jeans, a lacy knitted top, and new clogs. My hair had a body wave and was behaving itself beautifully. As I came up the steps, kids turned to stare at me. I didn't mind their stares. When I flashed them a grin, they smiled back timidly.

At the top of the steps a group of kids was standing together, talking and laughing, a whole group of cute girls and good-looking guys. As I walked toward them, they stopped talking and looked at me. Then one of the girls called out to me, "Are you the new kid who's just arrived from Hollywood?"

"Yes."

"We were waiting to meet you. Come on up."

If only that would happen, I thought as I drifted off to sleep. If only . . .

As it was, I got through the whole morning without anybody saying a word to me. I did have to ask someone where the women's room was, but that was it for conversation. At noon I took my lunch and wandered across campus to a big old oak tree. I sat down in its cool shade, rested my back against its trunk, and closed my eyes.

"Fought any good chickens lately?" came a voice beside me, and there was Mike, standing over me.

I sat up warily, wondering if he'd spread the story yet. "Ha, ha," I said, weary of the joke.

"Actually," said Mike, still grinning, "I came over to find out how it's going so far. You finding your way around OK?"

"Of course I am. I'm used to a school with three thousand kids, you know."

"Of course. I keep forgetting you're big time. You look so ordinary."

"You sure know how to flatter a girl!" I said. "What did you expect—pink hair?" I unwrapped my sandwich and took a bite.

"Well, I guess I'd better be going," he said

hesitantly and walked slowly away. I felt a sudden stab of guilt. Had he really been teasing me, or was he trying to be friendly? It was hard to tell.

As I watched him leave, a shadow fell across me. I looked up into the face of a truly gorgeous girl. She had long dark hair, flashing brown eyes, perfect makeup; she was wearing a dainty blue sundress with a little white jacket. She was beautiful, but she looked at me coldly.

"You new here?" she asked.

"Yes." She was probably one of the "in" kids—and she had actually come over to talk to me. But she certainly didn't look pleasant. I felt both scared and excited.

"I thought so," she said. "Otherwise you wouldn't be dumb enough to be sitting in my spot."

"Your spot?"

"Yeah. I eat my lunch here every day. Me and my friends. So move."

A group of kids was walking across the grass toward us. They looked like the kids from my fantasy the night before—great clothes, perfect hair. I had no intention of staying around and making a scene with people like that.

I stumbled to my feet, feeling my face flush scarlet. "I'm sorry," I muttered and turned to go.

"Hey," a voice yelled, and the girl and I turned around. There was Mike again, slouching against the back of a bench, watching us.

"You'd think twice about telling her off, Raven," he said, "if you knew her mother was a big Hollywood star." He turned on his heel and walked off.

Maybe I had been a little curt with Mike, but I didn't think I had *that* coming to me.

All afternoon I fumed. How could Mike do that to me? How dare he? I didn't really want anyone to know about me and my famous mother. Now this Raven would think I was a complete jerk. She'd probably also think I made the story up. What right did he have to start interfering with my life?

Of course, I thought miserably, I was the one who blurted it out to him about my mother, but he had made me mad.

I would have to cool it with Mike, I decided. Either I could be polite and start fresh or—or—I couldn't think what else, outside of avoiding him, and that seemed quite difficult to do. *Just calm down*, I finally told myself for the umpteenth time, and hold your tongue the next time you see him.

Chapter Six

The Valley of the Moon Marching Band met in the music room after school. I hung around in the doorway outside, clutching my clarinet, until Mr. Paolini noticed me. He was a podgy little man with a lot of white hair that stood out in all directions and made him look more like a mad scientist than a conductor.

"Come in, come in," he boomed in a voice that seemed too big for such a small person. "Don't just stand there propping up the wall. Now then, name and instrument!"

When I told him, his face broke into a big smile, as if I had told him I had arrived straight from the New York Philharmonic. "Clarinet, eh? That's wonderful, wonderful. We're short of clarinets this year, and those we have aren't worth a can of worms."

There were growls from the clarinet section, and I resigned myself to the fact that I was working with yet another of the famous Sonoma teases.

"OK, young lady, don't hold us up any longer, we're waiting to start," he said, patting me on the back. "Go and sit next to Shannon."

A pretty, dark girl smiled at me and moved her chair over to make space for mine.

"I hear you're the one who moved here from Hollywood," she whispered.

News certainly traveled fast in a small community.

She looked at me admiringly. "Did you meet many movie stars?"

"A few," I said, not wanting to sound like I was bragging.

"Did you ever meet Scott Baio?"

"I wish," I said shaking my head.

"Boy, I wish I could meet him one day," she said dreamily. "Isn't he cute?"

Mr. Paolini rapped on a desk with his baton. "Ladies and gentlemen, could we possibly get started?" he asked sweetly. "I really don't want to disturb your conversation, but I, for one, would like to get home before midnight tonight."

The kids smiled and picked up their instruments. Then the hard work started. Mr. Paolini seemed a jolly enough old man, but he certainly demanded perfection. If we made one little mistake, he would stop and cover his head with his hands, moaning in agony. "Mr. Sousa would turn over in his grave if he heard this," he would say, then sigh. "Now could we try it once more, and this time remember the B-flat?"

Mr. Paolini was helped out by a student conductor named Rick, who led the band when it was actually marching. He was much stricter than Mr. Paolini, and he didn't smile either. I just hoped he wasn't noticing how hard I had to struggle with my music—my clarinet skills were a bit rusty after a summer of no practice. Actually I faked it half the time, doing the fingering but not actually making any sound so nobody would hear if I hit a wrong note. Shannon noticed and looked across at me with a smile.

"They're hard pieces to begin with, aren't they?" she said reassuringly.

When at last practice was over, Shannon waited for me. "You know, I can't wait to go somewhere like Hollywood," she said. "There are no cute boys around here at all."

"I resent that remark and dismiss it as totally untrue," a boy's voice said behind us. By this time I recognized the voice and didn't even want to look around, but Shannon spun around at once.

"Mike Gibson, didn't your mother ever tell you it's rude to butt in to other people's conversations?"

Mike didn't seem to mind Shannon's outburst. He just went on grinning.

"What are you doing here, anyway?" I asked foolishly. Obviously he played in the band. I had a sinking feeling Mike was actually a ghost sent to haunt me.

"Just keeping an eye on you, like your grandmother said," he replied pleasantly. "I'm doing it for a Boy Scout merit badge."

"Don't you believe a word he says," Shan-

41

non said. "That's Mike Gibson, and he's the world's biggest tease."

"I know. I already found that out," I said. "And don't tell me he plays in the band."

"Unfortunately. He's the lead trombonist."

"Yeah. The band wouldn't even function without me. We'd have no oompah," Mike said. "And what's more, the trombones march right behind the clarinets, and I'm a devil with my slide."

"Charming, isn't he?" Shannon asked. "Now do you see why I said there are no cute boys here? I bet you didn't have to put up with boys like Mike in Hollywood."

"Oh, the boys are just as bad there," I said.

She sighed. "Really? I guess boys everywhere are a pain."

"That's what you say until one of them invites you to the homecoming dance," Mike said. He seemed to be enjoying the insulting banter.

"Well, I wouldn't go with *you*, that's for sure," Shannon said.

"And I wouldn't ask you," Mike retorted. "I already have my girl all picked out for homecoming this year."

Did I feel a quick stab of jealousy that Mike had a girl picked out for homecoming? I couldn't believe it myself, because I knew exactly the sort of boy I wanted to escort me to my first big dance. And it wasn't ordinary Mike Gibson!

When I got home from school, I found that

Grandma had a visitor. I heard two voices coming from the sitting room, voices that were raised in argument. I heard my grandmother shout something about a "stubborn old man." Naturally this made me very curious. Also I decided I had better go and see if she needed protection. So I crept up to the door and peeked in. My grandmother and another person were hunched over a table, glaring at each other. As I stood in the doorway, my grandmother caught sight of me, sat upright, and smiled.

"Oh, come in, Lisa. I'd like you to meet someone." I edged into the room—dying of curiosity—to find them bent over a game of checkers!

The old man rose to his feet as I came in. His face was as chubby and pink as a baby's, and his head was shiny and bald. When he stood up, I saw he was a big man.

"Lisa," my grandmother said, "I want you to meet Herbie Potter."

"So this is the famous granddaughter," Herbie said in a voice that squeaked like a rusty swing. "I've been wondering what you'd look like." He shook my hand so hard that he almost crushed it.

"Herbie is my greatest friend and rival," Grandma said.

I looked at him inquiringly. He smiled, sheepish. "That's right. We play checkers together, and we both hate to lose," he said, chuckling. "She's an awful stubborn old woman."

"And you're a scheming old man," she snapped.

"Scheming?" he sputtered. "Who distracted my attention so she could hop over four of my men?"

"That was perfectly fair," Grandma said. "I never resort to cheating like some people I could mention."

"And I'm never a sore loser, like some people *I* could mention," Herbie said triumphantly.

I began to realize that what had sounded like a fight was just their normal way of talking to each other.

"So how do you like our town, young lady?" Herbie asked in his squeaky voice.

"Very pretty," I said.

"A bit slow after the life you've been used to, I should imagine." He chuckled again.

"Oh, life wasn't so different there," I said. "We got up, went to school, did our homework. Just like here."

"But what about all those wild parties I read about?"

"They are just things that newspapers print when they haven't got anything better to say. I'm sure there are wild parties in Hollywood, but I bet some kids here are just as wild."

"Well, I guess that's true," Herbie said. "Sam Dwyer told me that a gang of kids broke into his liquor store last Saturday night. Took several cases of beer. That's how they knew it was kids. They left the money in the till and just took the beer. So I guess there's bad along with the good no matter where you are." He glanced over at the grandfather clock in the corner. "Well, I guess I'd better be going, Edith. Same time next week? Nice meeting you, young lady. Stay away from the wild ones, OK?"

He walked out chuckling.

I looked at my grandmother inquiringly.

"Oh, Herbie and I always play checkers on Wednesdays," she said. She sounded a bit flustered, as if I had caught her at something, and it did cross my mind that he was "courting" her, as she would have put it.

"I've got some cookies ready for you in the kitchen," she said, getting up. "Then you can tell me all about your first day at school."

Grandma sat down with me to keep me company while I ate my snack. I couldn't get over it. I was so used to eating—snacks, meals, anything—alone that it seemed almost strange, but believe me, I enjoyed it. All that attention!

Later I realized Grandma must have rearranged her life to have me come live with her. She took care of solitary chores while I was at school and saved the things we could do together until I got home. And with all the work to be done, we often spent entire afternoons together. Grandma didn't force herself on me, though. If I disappeared upstairs for a little privacy, she never called after me or disturbed me.

On the other hand, she didn't let me get

away without doing chores—or homework. She just made the chores a lot of fun. And she did allow herself time to see Herbie. I often wondered if it took a lot of planning and thought on Grandma's part to be such a good "mother" to me, or if it just came naturally. I also wondered if she resented any of it.

Anyway, on the afternoon of that first day of school, Grandma and I sat down together in her cool kitchen, and I told her all about my classes and band practice and Shannon. Even though I felt totally comfortable with her and even though I could talk to her like she was a friend, I left out the parts about the confrontations with Raven and Mike. I wasn't sure why. I just knew I wasn't ready to talk about them.

When I finished telling Grandma about me, I had this burning desire to ask her about Herbie, but I decided it might be prying. Grandma was always a good listener, but she never asked personal questions. So I kept my mouth shut.

We sat in companionable silence until Grandma said, "Well, ready to hit the tomato beds?"

"Ready," I said, and we set off to do our chores.

Chapter Seven

The next morning as I headed up the front steps into the building, I noticed a group of kids standing off to one side, looking at me. They were the big shots of my fantasy with Calvin Klein and Jordache labels on everything they wore. I was about to walk right past them when one of the girls called out, "Hi, Lisa!"

Then a couple of others said, "Hi, Lisa," too. I was almost too astounded to answer back, but I managed a weak, "Hi."

Then I saw Raven standing on the other side of the group. She sauntered toward me. "Hi, Lis. Want to join us for lunch today under the oak tree?" she asked, giving me a friendly smile.

I must have looked like a dummy, standing there with my mouth open, because the other kids laughed and crowded around me. But Raven was completely different from the person she had been the day before.

One girl looked at me with wide blue eyes. "Is it true what we heard—that you come from Hollywood?"

"And that your mother's a movie star?" someone else chimed in.

Part of me wanted to deny the whole thing: "Who me? No, I'm just plain old Lisa Daniels." But the other part whispered, "Are you crazy? You should at least *try* to make a few friends, and here's your opportunity. Tell them what they want to hear."

"That's right," I said in my best Hollywood voice, low and smooth like my mother's. "My mother is Lana Daniels."

For one horrible moment I worried that they would say, "Never heard of her." But instead they looked impressed.

"Wow, Lana Daniels!" the first girl said. "Are you kidding? How about that, Raven? You've seen *Bride of the Mummy* about a dozen times, haven't you? It's our favorite movie," she added for my benefit. "Every time it's on TV, we all get together to watch it."

"Yeah," said another girl. "Sometimes we throw *Bride of the Mummy* parties and come dressed up like mummies and stuff. Lana Daniels! I can't believe it!"

"Will you guys stop going on about Hollywood," said Raven, but I could tell she was impressed. She just didn't want to *look* impressed. It went against her role as big shot.

"Oh, come on, Raven, when do we get to meet a person who knows real live movie stars?" the girl responded. "And who's in *Bride* no less."

I understood how they felt about *Bride of*

the Mummy. It was the same way I felt about *Psycho.*

"Hey, Lisa, did lots of actors and actresses come to your house?" another girl asked.

"Did you ever get to meet Christopher Reeve?"

"Or Harrison Ford?"

The bell saved me from having to lie my way out of that one.

"We'd better go," one of the boys said. "We don't want a late slip this early in the year."

"You can tell us all about it at lunchtime, Lisa," Raven said, giving me her sweetest smile. She and her flock hurried off.

All through chemistry I tried to decide whether I should actually meet Raven for lunch. Part of me didn't want anything to do with the sort of girl who ignored you if you were nobody and made a fuss if you—or your mother—were somebody. But the other part argued that if I got accepted by the hot shots like Raven's gang, I'd be accepted by the whole school. And besides, nobody else had asked me to eat lunch with them. So at noon I turned up under the tree just as Raven arrived with her followers.

"Lisa," she said, giving me a smile right out of a toothpaste commercial, "I want you to meet the rest of the kids. This is Kathy, Dorette, Sabrina, Joe, Rusty, and Paul." She pointed to them in quick succession, so quick I didn't catch which name belonged to which. The three girls looked like clones of each other—blond hair, obviously styled with a blow dryer each morning, just the right amount of makeup, jean skirts, and short-sleeved polo shirts in various pastel colors. They all smiled like candidates for Miss Teenage America and said, "Hi, Lisa," in identical voices at the same time.

The boys were all big and husky, and I guessed they were on the football team. I wondered which one was Raven's. That question was soon answered for me when one of the girls—Dorette, I think—asked, "Where's Brad, Rave?"

"Oh, he had to see the coach about something," Raven said, sinking down to the grass.

"Football seems to be taking up a lot of his time these days," Kathy said knowingly.

"You're telling me," Raven said, and a flash of something not very nice crossed her face before she relaxed again.

"Hey, come on now, girls," Rusty said. I remembered Rusty because he was the red-headed one. "You know he wants to get that football scholarship to UC. The coach is doing everything he can to help him."

"Yeah, you're just going to have to be patient, loving, and understanding, Raven," Paul said sarcastically.

"Listen, guys," Raven said, "you know patient, loving, and understanding are not my strong points." The kids laughed.

"Lisa," Raven said, directing her attention to me, "don't ever date a football player. They do everything their coach tells them, and they put football before all else."

"I bet plenty of girls would be waiting to snap up Brad if you decided you were through with him," Kathy said. "Me for one. He is totally gorgeous."

"Hey, what about me?" Joe asked.

"You'll do until Brad's free," Kathy joked, patting his knee. "Then you can go on to Lisa. She doesn't have a boyfriend yet, and you're nice and steady and reliable."

"All right! What about it, Lisa?" Joe grinned. "Is it a date?"

I was sitting there, basking in the warmth of being part of that group. At my old school I had seen groups like theirs and never, ever been part of one. Whatever Raven's reasons were for wanting me, I was sure glad to be there.

After lunch I overheard Kathy and Dorette talking in the bathroom, obviously about me.

"Nice kid and not a bit pushy," Kathy commented.

Dorette answered, "Yeah, you'd never know she came from Hollywood."

I snuck out of the bathroom feeling ridiculously relieved.

The best part of the day happened after school. I was leaving the building when Raven called, "Hey, Lisa. Wait up. I'll walk with you." I was certainly glad of her company. My grandmother hadn't managed to find me a bike yet, and it was a long, boring walk home.

"OK, so tell me all about it," Raven said as soon as she caught up with me.

"About what?"

"Hollywood, of course. What's it like to meet all those famous people? Did movie stars really come to your house?"

I tried hard not to smile. I was even tempted to say, "I thought you weren't interested," but I was wise enough not to. I didn't think Raven was the sort of girl who liked to be made fun of. What could I say? That I was sure movie stars came to our house when I was a little kid, but I didn't remember? In those days people were either nice—they brought me presents—or not nice—they ignored me. The fact was, I hadn't seen a real live movie star in several years, just a few has-beens who hung around with my mother.

But that wasn't what Raven wanted to hear. And she would never find out the truth, whatever I said. So I told her about the Hollywood of my fantasies in which my mother was still rich and famous. ". . . and we had this fantastic party, and almost everybody came—"

"Even Matt Dillon?" Raven interrupted.

"I think so," I said, trying to look bored and vague about the whole thing. "I can't remember anymore."

"Wow," Raven said, "You can't even remember if Matt Dillon came! I know *I'd* remember."

"Well, it wasn't any big thing, really," I said. I was playing my part very well. She was eating it up. I was a big shot, and nobody was getting hurt by it. So why did I feel so rotten and mean?

"I can't wait to go somewhere exciting," Raven said. "I'd leave this dumb town now if I had any money. I mean, a town like this is dead. No life at all. The people are all a bunch of old fogies who always try to stop you from having a good time. I tell you, as soon as I get some money, I'm going to head straight for Hollywood."

I looked at Raven and saw her as she really was: not tough like she tried to be, but just a small-town girl who wanted more from life than her small town had to offer. Suddenly I felt really bad.

Terrific. Now look what you've done, I thought. You ought to tell her what it's really like. Tell her about all those girls who want to be in movies but end up working at Jack in the Box instead. Tell her about people like my mother, willing to do soap powder commercials just so people don't forget their faces. . . .

I was interrupted from these thoughts by Raven asking, "What I don't get is how come you ever left it? What would make you come to a dump like this?"

"My parents," I said bluntly. "They're separated. My mother wants to lead her own life, and my father has gone abroad. That left my grandmother."

"You, too?" she said sympathetically. "Mothers aren't all they're cracked up to be. But in your case I suppose that's the price you pay for fame."

We turned out of the square and onto a quiet side street. There was no sidewalk, and white dust rose under our feet.

"By the way," Raven said, "I meant to ask you about your clothes—"

"Don't say it," I interrupted. "They're terrible, right?"

"Well, I mean, they're not the sort of clothes I'd expect Lana Daniels's daughter to wear."

That put me in a difficult position. I didn't want to tell Raven about my mother and her spending and her debts, but I didn't want to make it sound like we were too poor to buy decent clothes for me, either.

"I do need some new ones," I said. "But I wanted to wait until I saw what the other kids were wearing. I guess I'll go shopping this weekend."

"Oh, can I come along?" Raven asked excitedly. "I like to help people pick out clothes."

"Sure," I said a little hesitantly, wondering what on earth made me say that and how I could get out of it. I didn't have a cent to spend. "I'll let you know when I'm going." Then another idea crossed my mind. Raven was the sort of kid who knew everything and knew everybody.

"Hey, Raven," I said. "I want to get a job. Do you have any ideas?"

"You? A job? How come?"

"Oh, I want to prove to my parents that I can stand on my own feet for a while," I answered casually. "I'm sixteen. I shouldn't have to write and ask them for money all the time."

"I would," Raven said. "If my parents were rich."

"You don't understand," I said. "I don't want to be known as Lana Daniels's daughter all my life. I want to be myself. *Lisa* Daniels."

"And getting a job would do that for you?"

"It would be a start."

We passed by a sweet-smelling honeysuckle bush. Raven pushed the branches away as if they didn't exist.

"I know of one job," she said. "It's in Fantasyland, a boutique on the square. They sell all sorts of gift junk—unicorns and rainbows and dragons. You know. Mrs. Costello used to have someone help her out on weekends, but the girl's gone off to college this fall. You want me to introduce you to Mrs. Costello on Saturday?"

I beamed at her. "That would be great. Thanks, Raven."

She shrugged her shoulders. "You're weird," she said. "You wouldn't catch me working if I didn't have to."

We stopped in front of my grandmother's house. "You want to come in and meet my grandmother?" I asked. "She bakes cookies."

"No kidding," Raven said and laughed. "I didn't think there were any grandmothers left who did that sort of thing. I thought they all did yoga and played racquetball and went jogging and took classes with old men."

I smiled. "Well, mine's the genuine old-fashioned kind."

"OK, let's go," she said. "This I gotta see."

Chapter Eight

I must admit I did have a quick pang of worry about letting Raven meet my grandmother. After all, Grandma was strict about things like politeness and makeup. But I need not have worried. I should have realized Raven was a born actress—or con-artist—and could turn on the charm whenever she wanted to.

"I'm very pleased to meet you, Mrs. Daniels," she said politely. "Lisa's told me so much about you, I feel I know you already."

"What a nice, well-mannered girl," my grandmother said after Raven had gone. "I'm glad you are making the right kind of friends."

"Sure," I said as I cleared away the cookie crumbs. I felt rather strange, torn in two directions. Part of me was glad Raven and my grandmother got along so well, the other part was uneasy because I knew Raven had been playacting for my grandmother. And yet who was the real Raven? Every time I saw her she seemed to be somebody else. But right then I was basking too much in the sunshine of her friendship to care.

That weekend three good things happened.

First, I went with Raven to meet Mrs. Costello at Fantasyland. It was a really cute little store built into an old stable in a tiny brick shopping mall, and it was full of the sort of things that were nearest and dearest to my heart. How could anyone else have known that all my life I had wanted to own a unicorn? Or back in the days when my pretending was more along the lines of princesses and magic, that I used to imagine taming a dragon?

I wanted that job so badly. To work among those cute, furry animals and delicate glass unicorns and fat stuffed dwarfs and rainbow mobiles would be one step away from heaven as far as I was concerned. But the way Mrs. Costello looked at me, dressed in my old jeans, I could tell she didn't think I was right for her store.

"Well, I don't know if I need somebody right now," she said. "Not somebody as young as you, I mean. After all, there is a lot of pressure working here, a lot of money to be handled." The way she looked at me indicated that some of it might go straight into my pocket.

Then Raven stepped in. Again I had to admire her way of handling people. She came across as the clean-cut, all-American cheerleader, and I came out of the store with a job. Starting in two weeks, I was to work Saturday and Sunday from noon until five at three dollars an hour. That would be thirty dollars a weekend. I felt incredibly rich.

On the strength of future wages I decided

to ask my grandmother to lend me some money after all. I don't know where my grandmother came up with the money, but she loaned me a lot more than was in her mad-money fund, and on Sunday I went with Raven and Kathy to buy some new clothes.

Raven was, as she had said, very good at choosing clothes. Under her supervision I got a new pair of jeans, a pair of corduroys, a lace blouse, and a mohair sweater that went with both pairs of pants. Then I got a neat-looking, plum-colored jacket with a lambskin lining to wear over them when the weather got colder. I knew this would eat up a hefty amount of pay, but it was worth it to see Raven's and Kathy's approving looks.

They came home with me and watched while I tried on the outfits for Grandma, who whole-heartedly approved of everything. "You look love-ly, Lisa," she said, and I basked in her support. She made me feel so *good*!

Then Kathy said, "Hey, Lisa, let me french braid your hair."

"Yeah," Raven said, jumping up to get a comb. "She's really good at it."

Kathy took about half an hour, but in the end I could see she had done a fantastic job. My hair, which is usually just average looking, was now wound around my head in one big braid, like a halo.

Then Raven got enthusiastic and decided to do my makeup for me, so that by the end of the afternoon I looked like a different person. Even I, examining myself critically in the mirror, had to admit I looked good. For a second I thought it was my mother's face that looked back at me from the glass. Then I showed Grandma, and she hugged me and cried, "Beautiful! My granddaughter—you're not a little girl anymore."

And Raven said, "Hey, Lisa, you're really pretty! I don't think I should let Brad meet you after all."

"Yeah, Lisa, why don't you try out for cheerleader?" Kathy said. "I bet you'd make it. You've got such long legs. We're all cheerleaders, and it's really fun. We have these cute red-and-white uniforms, and we get to ride on the bus with the boys and go to all the games!"

"Yeah, why don't you try out?" Raven asked, but she didn't sound as keen as Kathy.

I tried to picture it. I imagined myself in a red sweater and a short, red-and-white pleated skirt, pom-poms beside me. I was sitting in the girls' locker room with Raven and Kathy and nine other girls, putting on short, white socks and sneakers.

"Ready, everybody?" Raven cried, springing to her feet.

"Ready," we all cried, springing along with her.

We formed a line and ran out onto the football field. Two cute football players fainted at the sight of us. The crowd cheered and clapped.

A newspaper photographer snapped a series of action shots. Accustomed as we were to all this attention, we launched into our first cheer.

"Lisa," someone called.

It was one of my fans. . . .

Wait. No, it was Raven. And I was daydreaming again.

"I *said*," Raven repeated crossly, looking at me oddly, "are you going to try out?"

I tried to clear my head. I didn't want Raven thinking I was weird.

"I'd like to, but I've already signed up for marching band," I said, "and there's no way I could do both."

"Gee, that's a shame," Raven said, and I got the definite feeling she was relieved.

However, all this attention was quite new to me. At Hollywood High I'd just been Lisa Daniels, who somehow didn't take after her gorgeous mother. I got invited to a few parties, but nobody ever saw me as a threat to anyone. I went to dances and danced and had a good time, but no boy ever looked at me as if I was the one special girl in the world. In fact, I had never really had a boyfriend. A few boys had asked me out, but I had such a clear vision of how "Mr. Right" would look that I had turned them down. And I was still waiting for Mr. Right to show up.

I decided on my Mr. Right way back when I was about eight. In those days, my mother was still acting like the Big Movie Star and inviting lots of people to our house. She used to dress me up in my cutest, frilliest dress and have me pass the hors d'oeuvres. I think she did it so people would say, "This can't be *your* daughter, Lana. You look much too young to have a big daughter like this!" Because that is often what they did say, along with a lot of other meaningless things.

One evening I was standing with my tray of stuffed mushrooms, feeling bored and tired and wishing I could sneak upstairs to watch TV, when I looked across the room. The room was so hazy with smoke that my eyes were watering. I rubbed them a couple of times to make sure I was seeing properly, for across the room, on the other side of the crowd, was the most gorgeous man I had ever seen. A prince! He was leaning against the wall with a drink in one hand, looking quite relaxed and far away. He had lots of dark curls and a straight nose and a little dimple in his chin and big dark eyes—and he looked as bored as I felt. When our eyes met, his lit up with an amused twinkle, and he gave me a big wink that clearly said, "Listen to all the nonsense these other people are talking. You and I both know that they're all phony, don't we?"

I never did find out his name, and I never saw him again, but from then on, whenever I dreamed of meeting Mr. Right, he always looked just like that man. Eventually I invented a classic daydream in which I, sixteen and beautiful, waited alone on one side of a crowd. Then I would see him across the room. Our eyes would meet, and he would smile that wonderful smile. He would make his way through the crowd to me. "We both seem to find this party equally boring," he would say, "so why don't we take a walk?"

He had set the standard for all future boyfriends. When I have a boyfriend, he will be really special, I had decided back in junior high. I'm not going to go with just anybody for the sake of having a boyfriend. I'm going to wait for the right boy. Well, I was still waiting!

At five o'clock the doorbell rang. My grandmother had gone out—to take some freshly picked vegetables to a friend who was a shut-in—so I answered it.

I opened the door and froze immediately. I was standing face to face with the most fantastic boy I had ever seen. He was very tall and looked very strong. Even his loose sweatshirt could not hide his muscular shoulders. He had a mass of dark curls and a straight nose. He stood there looking at me with big brown eyes.

"Hi, there," he said in a voice that was a deep rumble.

I tried to say hi back, but I think my lips were paralyzed. I know I was clutching hard at the doorknob to keep myself from falling.

"Is this the Daniels residence?" he asked.

I finally managed to nod. I was willing him

63

to say, "I've been sent over to escort Lisa Daniels to a dance this evening."

But he didn't. Instead he said, "I was told I could find Raven Delgado here."

"Raven?" I heard myself stammer. "You want Raven?"

He smiled a gorgeous, warm smile that made my knees go even weaker. "Yes, I was supposed to meet her at seven, but I—I couldn't wait any longer. Would you tell her Brad's here?"

Chapter Nine

All the next week I went through agony and ecstasy. Ecstasy because Brad was everything I had ever dreamed of in a boy—and agony because he belonged to Raven, not me.

You can't take away Raven's boyfriend, I would tell myself severely. Look how nice she's being to you. If it weren't for her, you wouldn't know anybody in school. You'd have no job and no clothes. I didn't dare add that I believed Raven would probably be highly dangerous if I wound up on her wrong side.

But nothing could stop me from thinking about him. And I thought about him practically every minute—the way he smiled, the pleasant way his voice rumbled, the way one stray curl fell down onto his forehead. Several teachers had to ask me if I was paying attention in class. Of course I wasn't.

I tried very hard to concentrate in class. After all, I wanted to be known as a good student, but there was no way I could stop Brad from creeping back into my thoughts. I imagined him sitting next to me in chemistry, giving me a reassuring wink when the test was hard, walking beside me down the hall with his hand firmly holding mine so the whole world knew I was his girl. I pictured him waiting, to walk me home as I came out of school.

"Lisa!" he called as he caught sight of me. He was sitting on the hood of a car, and he waved to attract my attention.

"Hi," I called back breathlessly and ran down the school steps toward him as he slid off the car.

He gathered me lightly in his arms and gave me a gentle kiss on the lips.

We looked at each other for a minute but didn't let go.

"Been waiting long?" I asked coyly.

"It always seems long when I'm waiting for you, baby," he replied.

I kissed him on the cheek. "Oh, *Brad*."

"I saw Raven while I was waiting," he said in an undertone.

"Oh, yeah?"

"Yeah. She looked dreadful. Like she hadn't slept in weeks."

"It may take her awhile to get over this," I said. "It's sort of like overthrowing a government."

"Well, let's not worry about her. We have each other, darling, and that's what's important."

I melted into his arms. . . .

When this daydream ended, I was relieved to find I had come through it unscathed. That particular time I had chosen to daydream while classes were changing, which was not bright.

There was the danger of a collision, of book dropping, and of falling down the stairs.

Even so, my thoughts returned to Brad. There had to be some way I could make it happen. Surely Raven wasn't the sort of girl who stayed with one boy for long. She had said the other day that she was getting tired of waiting around while Brad thought of nothing but football. Perhaps he was getting tired of her, too. Perhaps, if he noticed the right girl at the right moment . . . He *had* looked at me approvingly when we first met at my front door.

All I needed was the chance to meet him, to get to know him, to be alone with him. But whether he was busy practicing football or whether Raven kept him well away from the rest of us, I didn't see him once all week. Which meant I looked forward to Friday night and the first football game more and more every moment.

In the band I was working hard for that first game. Most of the other kids had been in the marching band the past year and knew all the routines. But I had to concentrate really hard to learn all the complicated wheels and formations. In fact, I had to keep a very close eye on Shannon, who marched beside me, if I didn't want to get lost.

"Phew," I sighed after practice one night. "I'm exhausted." I flopped down beside my clarinet case. "I didn't realize marching band would be so tiring. Remind me to go out for the football team next year. I bet their practice is much easier than this."

Shannon laughed. "Oh, it's really not bad when you know what you're doing," she said. "It's just that all the moves are new to you. Pretty soon you'll be hearing Rick's voice yelling at you in your sleep. Right—Wheel—Three—Four—Five—Six—Seven—HALT!"

"The problem is," I said as I took my clarinet apart, cleaned it, and put it in its case, "we have to play music and march at the same time. That makes it twice as hard. I'm trying to concentrate on counting the steps in the right wheel, at the same time I'm trying to read the notes to play. I never was that hot at sight-reading. But sight-reading and moving my feet at the same time, well, that's just impossible!"

Shannon snapped her clarinet case shut and got up. "Come on, Lisa. Don't worry about it. It was the same for all of us when we joined. Just think about all those gorgeous football players who'll be running past us."

"Don't make things any more complicated for me," I said and sighed. "If I can't think of marching and playing at the same time, I sure can't think of marching, playing, *and* football players!"

Rick drilled us like an army all week, and by Friday night I had at least some idea of what I was supposed to be doing. As we got into our uniforms that night, I was feeling both excited and nervous. Grandma and Herbie would be in the stands watching, which pleased me *and* scared me. But any worries I might have had about not knowing the music or the steps were pushed into the very back of my mind by the thought that in just thirty minutes I was going to see Brad again.

Our uniforms were real parade-type band uniforms. We looked like little toy soldiers—red suits with white trim and lots of gold braid. Mine fitted me perfectly, and I commented to Shannon about how lucky I was that someone had left who was just my size.

She looked at me admiringly. "Wow, you look as if you were poured into that," she said. "I bet none of the boys will pay attention to the game tonight!"

I felt quite daring when I put on a little blusher and mascara. But Shannon shook her head and came over to me. "You need much more than that," she said. "Those lights make everyone look awfully pale. Here, let me do it for you."

She gave me two bright cheeks and thick, black lashes, making me look even more like an old-fashioned toy soldier, especially when I stuck the little red hat with the white feather on top of my head. Shannon adjusted it for me.

"There," she said. "Now get out there and play. The band's all ready to go."

We were almost the last two to join the band lineup. I walked past Mike, who gave me a wink, and took up my place behind the flutes.

"OK, you guys," Rick barked, "make it snappy tonight. I want it crisp, understand? Good clean lines and no wrong notes. Are you all ready?"

"Yes," we chorused.

He raised his baton. The drums began, their marching rhythm nearly splitting our ears in that confined hallway.

"Band, forward march," Rick yelled.

We emerged from the hallway into the brightly lit stadium. A cheer went up from the spectators that made my heart leap as though I was doing something important and special for once. I wondered what Grandma was thinking.

Then Rick raised his baton again, and we all burst into the theme from *Rocky*. We had practiced it all week, and I knew it well, but it had never sent shivers down my spine before. That night was different, maybe because we were playing it for hundreds of people, playing it for our team to win. I almost felt as if I were a soldier marching into battle.

I'm part of this, I thought. I belong. It was fantastic, a feeling I had never experienced before.

We marched the full length of the field, divided, wheeled in opposite directions, crossed in mid-field, and met up again down where the players were due to appear. It all went without a hitch.

Then we changed to the theme from *Superman*, and the procession came out. First, the cheerleaders, rushing ahead and waving. Raven was in the middle, looking more gorgeous than ever in her little red-and-white pleated skirt and red T-shirt. She ran ahead of the others and did a couple of cartwheels. She looked like she was flying. Then the other girls did cartwheels, too, but not nearly so well as Raven.

"And now, ladies and gentlemen," the announcer yelled. "Presenting last year's North Coast champions—unbeaten—the Valley of the Moon Football Team!" He began to name the players as they ran out one by one, all looking like giants in their football padding. I heard him say, "And running back, Brad Sorensen." A great cheer went up from the bleachers as Brad flashed past me.

Suddenly I had a thought: tonight is the night. Tonight is what I have been waiting for all my life. Mr. Right will notice me—and he'll forget all about Raven.

Rick gave the command again, and we marched down the field behind the players. I felt as if I were floating on air. I could see it all so clearly, as clearly as a vision. Brad would be running with the ball. He'd make the touchdown right where I was standing. He'd place the ball triumphantly a few yards from my feet. Then he'd look up, and his eyes would meet mine. "Lisa," he'd whisper. "Wait for me after the game," and he wouldn't even notice the crowd going wild. . . .

The crowd certainly was making noise. They were laughing. I looked around to see what was so funny. Shannon was no longer beside me. Then I saw who was making them laugh. Me! The rest of the band had wheeled off to the left. I had wheeled off to the right. I was all alone under those lights with all those people watching me. Oh, Grandma, I thought. Then, oh, *Brad*. Me and my stupid daydreams. Of all the times not to pay attention, I had to pick that night.

I wanted to throw my clarinet down and run away, but I made myself keep in step. I pretended to play my clarinet, but actually nothing came out. I was shaking too much to blow. Suddenly I was aware of someone beside me.

"Left, right, left wheel," came the familiar voice, and Mike's trombone lined up with me.

"Keep up with me, keep in time," he said. "We'll make it look like a planned move. They'll never know."

"But they're laughing," I said hopelessly.

"We'll make them stop laughing," he said. "We'll show them some fancy stuff."

I could hardly leave him alone at one end of the field, could I? So I marched with him. We did a couple of wide circles before we intersected the main band coming up in wide formation for the final number. Several people clapped as we took our positions, and I began to hope that at least *somebody* would not know I had just made a fool of myself.

But I knew I couldn't face Rick. Rick was very hard on us. Much worse than Mr. Paolini.

The others called him sergeant major, and with good reason. I wasn't going to wait around to hear what he would yell at me. As soon as the band marched to its position behind the field, I quietly slipped up into the stands and ran for the band room, where I could be alone.

The band room was dark, and I didn't even bother to find the light switch. I stumbled against the desks. I kicked a music stand, and it toppled to the floor with a metallic crash, scattering music sheets. Then my hands closed on the secure woodenness of a chair, and I sank down onto it. Until now I had not cried. I had been too scared to do anything except escape. Now I felt the tears stinging my eyes. *Why did my imagination run away like that?* I'd have to learn to control it. It never got me anywhere but in trouble.

Stupid, I said to myself bitterly. Stupid, stupid. Once more the great Lisa Daniels did her great show-stopping performance and ended up looking like a fool. And what for? Because she was trying to pretend impossible things could happen. I slumped forward and buried my head in my hands. I felt my hat slide off sideways and thump onto the floor. I didn't even bother to look for it.

Why did I pretend that? I asked myself. I knew darn well Brad would never look at me. I wasn't Raven. I was nothing like her. I was only ordinary. A terrific-looking guy like Brad wouldn't take a second glance at a nobody like me! I had to face it. I was not my mother and I never would be.

I started to sob. Loudly. I tried to stop myself, to tell myself someone might hear and come to see what the problem was, and then I'd have to explain, but the sobs kept coming anyway.

I didn't hear anyone come in until I felt a strong arm around my shoulder.

I jumped. "Sorry," said Mike's voice beside me. "Here. You sound like you could do with this." He handed me a box of tissues.

"Thanks," I said, trying to stifle the sobs and hiccuping instead. "I'll be all right. You better get back to the band. They'll miss you."

"They'll miss you, too," he said gently.

"I can't go back there. They'll all laugh at me."

"No, they won't. They know you hardly had any time to learn the routines. They'll understand that you turned the wrong way."

"But I looked so stupid. I can't face them."

Mike stroked my hair. "Look, Lisa," he said, "you're going to have to see them all in school anyway. If you go back tonight and go on playing as if nothing happened, they'll admire you and know you've got guts. I bet they'll never even mention it again. But if you run away tonight, they'll giggle about it behind your back for weeks. And besides"—he smiled his cheeky grin—"it's like falling off a horse. You have to get right back on, or you lose your nerve."

"But I must look terrible," I said. I could feel my thickly applied mascara running into my thickly applied blusher.

Mike peered at me critically. "Yeah, you do look pretty terrible, even without the light," he said. "But I'll walk you over to the bathrooms, and you can wash that junk off your face. Come on." And he held out his hand to me.

"Wait a minute," I said, "I have to find my hat." We scrabbled around together on the floor, separated, came together again, and bumped heads just as we both called, "I found it." Then we laughed.

"That's better," Mike said. He took my hand and helped me up.

"Come on, or we'll miss halftime, and Rick really will be mad."

We walked across the deserted school yard. Mike's hand felt warm and reassuring. I remembered how my father used to hold my hand when I was very small and scared of the dark. It was the same reassuring feeling that I felt now.

"Mike," I said, "thanks for everything: for rescuing me on the field and for being so nice."

He squeezed my hand. "That's OK. I'm a nice guy. And besides, anybody who gets attacked by chickens needs looking after."

Mike waited patiently for me as I scrubbed violently at my awful, blotchy, tear-streaked, mascara-stained face. It took quite a while, but at last I came out clean and scrubbed and definitely feeling better.

"Come on," he said, grabbing my hand again. "How can it take so long to wash your face?" He dragged me into a run.

"What I don't understand," Mike said at last, "is how you didn't notice you were marching the wrong way sooner. You were almost at the other end of the field by the time I spotted you."

I felt myself blushing as I tried to come up with a good, logical explanation for something quite unexplainable. "I was daydreaming," I said miserably. "I guess I just got carried away."

"That's all right," Mike said, squeezing my hand again. "Happens to the best of us."

"But it happens to me more often," I complained.

I slowed Mike down to a fast trot and then to a stop.

"Want to tell me about it?" he asked.

I groped for words. "I'm *always* daydreaming!" I exploded at last. "And it always gets me in trouble. But I can't seem to stop."

Mike looked at me seriously. "Some psychologists say daydreaming is healthy." He paused. "Others say it's an escape from real life. Maybe you just have a good imagination, though. What were you daydreaming about?"

I blushed—I was sure of it. At any rate, my face grew hot.

"Or perhaps I should ask, '*Who* were you daydreaming about?'"

My face grew hotter.

"Anyone I know?" Mike asked, teasing.

When I wouldn't say anything, Mike began grinning like crazy. Oh, *shoot*, I thought. Without saying a word, I've put my foot in my mouth.

Chapter Ten

Mike was absolutely right. Going back to the band was the best thing I could have done. With Mike holding my hand firmly—to prevent me from running away at the last minute—it was not nearly so bad as I had imagined. People around me took one look at my blotchy face and felt sorry for me. I heard a few giggles, but no out-and-out teasing.

Shannon turned and gave me a big smile. Peter, who played the drums, winked as I walked past, and even Rick, when I humbly apologized to him, growled, "Forget it. It's no big deal. No one could learn the whole routine in one week." And later that night Grandma said, "It looked like a very difficult routine. At least you got part of it right. And then you faced up to it later. That was hard to do. I'm very proud of you." She just wouldn't let me get down on myself!

Of course, it wasn't easy to forget about my mistake. I sweated as I lay in bed that night and went over and over it in my mind. Not all the kids at school would be quite as understanding as the band had been. But I had Raven on my side, and I had Mike, and probably not many kids would even remember the incident. However, on Monday when a couple of boys made dumb wisecracks about losing my way at school, Raven took over.

"Listen," she said. "How come your mouth is bigger than your brain? You just spread the word to all your dumb friends that if anyone mentions Friday night again, the football team will be waiting for him on the way home."

Raven was very impressive, like something out of a gangster movie. The way she sounded I didn't doubt for a minute she would and could set the football team on someone.

So I basked in Raven's protection. And then there was Mike. Mike had clearly decided it was not safe to let me out in the world alone anymore. After all, who knew what stupid thing I would do next? So without asking permission, he took over as my protector and bodyguard. He followed me around school. He didn't talk to me much, but he was there, just hanging around in the background.

"Here's your Secret Service man again," Raven would tease.

My feelings about Mike were mixed. I had to admit it was nice to have someone watching over me, like a guardian angel. Nobody had ever done that before. When I had lived with my parents, they had both been too busy with their own lives to worry about mine.

"I'm going over to Wendy's house, OK?" I

used to ask, and they would say, "Fine," as they rushed out of the door.

Grandma cared about me, of course, but she wasn't very strict, and I could tell she was making an effort to "give me some space" and not tie me down with a lot of restrictions right away.

Mike, though, had taken over as my self-appointed big brother. But I wasn't one hundred percent sure I wanted a big brother. At least not all the time. For one thing, it was kind of hard to meet any boys when Mike kept popping up like a jack-in-the-box every few seconds. For another, it was painfully obvious that Mike and Raven did not get along. If he showed up, she left and took her gang with her. Most of the time I'd rather have been with Raven if I'd had the choice.

"What's Mike Gibson's problem?" Raven asked me one day. We were all sitting eating lunch under our oak tree. It was a perfect fall day, warm and sunny, but the leaves were just beginning to turn yellow, and there was a hint of clouds over the hills, something we hadn't seen all summer.

"What do you mean?" I asked.

"I mean why is he acting so weird? Every time I look up, there he is peeking at us from behind a bush. Is he trying out for the CIA or something?"

I shrugged. "No, he's just keeping an eye on me, I guess."

"*Why?* Is he madly in love with you and too shy to speak? Or is he too jealous to let you out of his sight?"

"Are you kidding? He's my next-door neighbor, and my grandmother asked him to keep an eye on me. I guess he just took her a little too seriously, that's all."

"I wonder," Raven said thoughtfully. "Mike Gibson doesn't seem the type who would go to all that trouble for a girl if he wasn't interested. . . ."

Then she and the others gave each other a knowing look, and I blushed before I could stop myself.

The next day I found the letter. I always collected the mail from our box on my way home from school. I did that every day, hoping for something from my parents. I'd been away nearly four weeks, and so far all I had had was one postcard of the Eiffel Tower in Paris, with "Love, Dad" scribbled on the back of it. I didn't really expect anything from my mother. She loathed writing letters, and she only remembered my existence when the spirit moved her. Still, I was always hopeful.

But today there was a letter for me! Not from my parents but unstamped and with only my name on the front. I ripped it open right there beside the oleander bushes. I was half expecting an invitation to a party. At home unstamped letters were always party invitations.

But after the first couple of words, I realized this was no invitation:

Dear Lisa,

I have been thinking about you day and night since we met. I want to tell you how I feel about you, but every time I see you I lose my nerve. Please tell me you like me, and say you'll go with me.

Until tomorrow,

Mike

I stood there on the gravel of the driveway, not moving, not seeing. Mike. Mike? That was the last thing in the world I had expected. Of course Mike had paid a lot of attention to me, but it was only the attention of a friend or of a big brother for a little sister. There had been no sign he was interested in me as a girl. He had held my hand, put his arm around me, but it had felt like a brother's hand and a brother's arm. Had it really felt different to him? I found it hard to believe. Mike didn't come across as the sort of boy who would be too shy to tell a girl he liked her. After all, I only lived next door. He could easily come and see me alone if he was afraid of talking at school. And the letter sounded so stiff and formal. Not at all like the Mike I thought I knew. Then I remembered Raven's remark. She had said he must be hanging around for a reason, for something besides just keeping an eye on me.

I walked up the path to the front door. The smell of baking came down the hall from the kitchen. I wanted to creep straight up to my room, but at that moment my grandmother came out of the kitchen with floury hands, a floury apron, and flour flecking her hair and glasses. She looked startled when she saw me.

"Oh, Lisa, it's you. I didn't hear you come in," she said. "How was school?"

"Fine," I said, not up for a conversation.

She peered at me through her floury lenses. "Are you feeling all right? You look a little pale to me."

"I'm fine," I said. "Just tired."

"You're not used to all this walking," said Grandma. "I really must make an effort to find you a bike. Why don't you go upstairs and have a little rest? I'll call you when this last batch of bread is done." She bustled back into the kitchen.

I went up the stairs slowly. My shoes felt as if they had lead in them. When I got to my room, I tried to rest but couldn't; instead, I paced up and down like a caged animal.

What was I going to do about Mike? It seemed so unfair. All my life I had dreamed of having a special boy—Mr. Right—feel that way about me, but Mike wasn't Mr. Right.

I knew whom I would have liked that letter to be from. If only I had come home and found a letter that said,

I never get a chance to see you at school because Raven's always around. But I think about you night and day. Meet me tomorrow under the big oak tree after school.

Brad

Then I saw myself walking across that field, wondering if he would show up. When I got near the tree, I saw he was already there, leaning against the trunk in deep shadow. His eyes lit up, and he flashed me that fabulous smile. "I knew you would come," he murmured. "I couldn't wait any longer. We may be hurting Raven, but we were fated to be together. . . ."

At that moment I turned around and bumped straight into the dresser, knocking over all the junk I kept on it. Several bottles crashed to the floor.

"Lisa," my grandmother called. "Are you all right?"

"I'm fine, Grandma, I just knocked something over," I called back. "No damage done."

Just my stupid daydreaming getting in the way again, I wanted to say.

So much for the great romantic scene, I thought sadly. That was not going to happen. Not now, not ever. I was stuck with Mike and with a situation I didn't know how to handle.

The trouble was I liked Mike. I was grateful to him. I was glad to have him around. But I wanted him as my brother, not as my boyfriend.

How can I tell him *that*? I wondered. I

paused and stood at the window. To my left I saw the wire of the famous chicken coop and the trees in Mike's yard beyond. How can I say anything without hurting him?

It was a problem I could share with nobody. Raven and her friends would only laugh, or worse still, tease me—or Mike. The only other person I could talk things over with was Grandma, and I didn't know if it was quite fair to Mike to discuss it with her. I mean, if I had written him a letter, I wouldn't want him discussing it with his mother.

Why can't I be a bit more like Raven? I thought. I bet she wouldn't care whose feelings she hurt. But I do care. I know how it feels to be hurt and rejected, and I don't want to do that to anyone else.

Chapter Eleven

I couldn't get Mike out of my mind all evening. He haunted me all through my homework. At supper my grandmother commented that I was unnaturally quiet and hoped I wasn't coming down with something. She mentioned that two families at church had stomach flu and asked if I was getting cramps. I assured her I was fine, glad for her concern, but I couldn't stop brooding. After the dishes had been done, Grandma and I stared at one dumb TV program after another; I was unwilling to go upstairs and shut myself in the silence of my room where I would have to think. That night my sleep was full of troubled dreams, and in the morning I was no nearer to knowing what I was going to say to Mike. It was clear I would have to face him sometime. After all, he would expect an answer to his letter. He would be waiting for me and hoping.

After lunchtime I met him coming along the walkway between the main building and the music room.

"Hi," he said cheerfully. "How's it going today?"

He looked so carefree and relaxed that I was thrown into confusion even more. Either Mike was a good actor and could hide his feelings or—suddenly another thought flashed through my mind. Was this only one of his jokes? I knew what a terrible tease he was. I knew he was famous for his jokes at school. Would he do something like this for a laugh?

So what on earth do I do now? I worried. Do I ignore it completely? No, I decided. I'd better find out. Just in case the note was serious.

"Mike," I said, "you and I have got to talk."

"OK, sure," he said uneasily. "Talk away."

"Somewhere private," I said.

"OK," he said again, looking more worried than ever. "How about the bike shed. It's private in there."

We walked across to the bike shed in silence. Neither of us looked at the other.

"Now," he said when we stepped into the cool shadow of the shed roof, "what's the problem?"

"Don't you know?" I asked suspiciously.

"Know what?"

"You must know why I want to talk to you."

"No, I—I really don't."

"The note—" I said, hesitating.

"The note?"

"Yes, I got it last night. I thought it over very carefully all evening. I've been trying to find a way to tell you nicely that it wouldn't work."

"It wouldn't?"

I thought Mike sounded more confused than hurt.

"No, Mike. I like you very much as a friend, but I can't go steady with you."

"You what?" Mike's eyes flew wide open, more startlingly blue than ever.

"I—I wish I could, but I can't. You do understand, don't you?"

"Let me get this straight," he said, running a hand through his hair. "You got a note asking you to go steady with me—"

"Oh, come on, Mike," I said impatiently. "It had your name on it. If this is your idea of a joke—"

"Lisa," he said, looking straight at me. "I didn't send any note."

Color flooded into my cheeks. "You didn't? But . . ." I stood there wishing that a tornado would touch down and suck me up into it and not let me go until we were over Taiwan or the Ukraine.

He smiled at me kindly. "Lisa, you should know me better than that by now. If I wanted to ask a girl to go with me, I'd come right out and say it. I wouldn't send any note."

"But it was in my mailbox last night, and it was signed Mike. Who else could have sent it?"

"I have a vague idea," Mike said, frowning.

"You do? Who?"

"Your friend Raven."

"Raven? Why on earth would she do a mean thing like that?"

"For a laugh. Raven's a great one for laughs. And she'd love to have one at my expense."

"I can't believe that," I said angrily. "Even if Raven wanted to play a mean trick on you, why would she play it on me, too? I'm her friend. She'd know it would make me look like an idiot."

"Raven only has one friend, and that's herself," Mike said dryly. "You'll find that out soon enough."

I turned on him. "Look, Mike, Raven's been very nice to me since I came here. She has defended me, helped me get a job, and taken me shopping. She wouldn't do a thing like this to me. You've got a chip on your shoulder about her. What did she do? Turn you down once?"

"Are you kidding? I'd no more take Raven out . . ." His voice trailed off as he searched for words. "No, I just don't like Raven. And she doesn't like me because I know her too well. Because I know her for what she really is. And I won't have anything to do with her."

"Well, I'm going to ask her about this right now," I said hotly. "And then I hope you'll have the decency to apologize when you find out you're wrong."

"If I'm wrong," Mike said calmly, "I'll apologize." He turned and walked out into the sunlight.

Raven wasn't under the elm tree. I found her sitting with the gang on the front steps of the school. It suddenly occurred to me that Raven was never alone. I always saw her in the middle of a group.

"Hi, Lis," she called out and waved.

I walked to her, but I didn't sit down. "Do you have a minute?" I asked. "I'd like to speak with you in private."

"Oooh, secrets," she said, jumping up. "I love secrets. Don't go away everybody. We'll be right back."

She followed me across the front lawn until I felt we were out of earshot.

"Raven," I said, feeling awkward about taking the upper hand with her, "I have to ask you something."

"OK. Ask away."

"I got a note last night. I thought it was from Mike Gibson. But when I talked to him about it today—"

"Oh, what did he say?" Raven butted in, with a big grin on her face. "Was he mad?"

"Then you know about the note?" I asked.

"Sure," she said. "I wrote it. Well, we all wrote it, but it was my idea. Was Mike really mad?"

"No, he wasn't mad. I was," I said. "And I still am. How could you do a thing like that? You made me look like a fool. I thought you were my friend."

"Hey," Raven said, still smiling, "it was only a joke, you know. Just like the kind Mike likes to play himself."

"But he doesn't hurt people," I said bitterly.

Raven's smile faded. Finally. "Come on, Lisa, where's your sense of humor?"

"I'm afraid my sense of humor doesn't include making fun of my friends," I said.

"Hey, you two, quit all this secret stuff and get back over here," Dorette called.

Raven's entourage was getting restless.

"Lisa's sore about our little joke," Raven called back.

"Oh, come on, Lisa," Dorette said, smiling just as Raven had. "We only did it for your own good, you know."

"My own *good*? What's that supposed to mean?" I said frostily.

"Oh, you know," Kathy joined in. "After all, you don't have a boyfriend yet." She snickered. "And we just wanted to get you two together," Dorette added, snickering along with Kathy.

"You're *perfect* for each other," Kathy said. "You should go together. You were *meant* for each other." They all laughed.

"I'm glad you're all so concerned about me," I said, trying to keep my voice calm and even, "but I don't need anyone to choose my boyfriends for me. So in the future stay out of my private life. If I want your help, I'll ask for it."

I stomped off. I realized as I went that I might have lost them as friends, but just then I wasn't sure I wanted friends like that. Mike was right. They had only done it for a laugh.

Chapter Twelve

That night there was a special on TV called "The Golden Years of Hollywood." Grandma and I watched it together. I saw it through a haze of foul humor. Toward the end they said a few words about my mother and showed her in a scene from one of her earlier pictures, a western. She looked incredibly young and pretty and not in the least like me.

The next morning I went to school still in a bad mood. Raven's trick smarted. In fact, it burned. I knew I needed friends, but I had to decide how badly. I was beginning to think Raven and her followers weren't worth it.

I walked into the building, and there was the gang hanging around in their usual place. They all sprang into action when they saw me.

"Oh, hi, Lisa. Did you see your mom on TV last night?" Dorette called.

"She looked so pretty," Kathy said, "and I was saying to Dorette that you really look a lot like her."

I didn't say anything.

Dorette and Kathy came to walk on either side of me. "You're not still mad about that silly joke, are you?" Dorette asked. "Raven feels bad about it. She didn't realize you'd be so upset."

I looked across at Raven. She gave me a sort of sheepish smile. "We're always playing jokes on each other, Lis," she said. "I guess that just shows we think of you as one of the kids now."

"Please warn me the next time you're going to think of me as one of the kids," I said stiffly. "I like to be prepared."

They all laughed as if that was terribly funny.

"I hope we all get to meet your mother sometime," Dorette said as we walked into class. "Raven's just dying to. She was so worried when she thought she'd made you mad."

So that's what this is all about, I thought. They just want to be sure they meet my famous mother. The experience left me with an incredibly bad taste in my mouth.

So I found it quite easy to act cool toward them all week. They did try extra hard to be nice, though, which made me think perhaps they did feel a little guilty about the joke after all. And every time I decided to drop them as friends, I'd look across the school yard at that big mass of strangers and think, just who else do I know, anyway? Only Mike, and I was going out of my way to avoid him. I blushed every time I thought of that embarrassing scene.

That weekend I started work at Fantasyland.

I had been looking forward to it, to being among all those adorable animals, and to the money as well; but to tell the truth, I was scared of Mrs. Costello. She looked as if she ought to be the head of a center for juvenile delinquents. She was big and broad and had the sort of face that registered disapproval. I wondered why someone like her would want to own a fantasy store instead of working as a prison guard.

So my first weekend at the store was very uneasy. I was dying to touch and look at all the wonderful things, to rearrange the unicorns and take a peek at the advanced Dungeons and Dragons games. But I was very conscious of Mrs. Costello hovering in the background, about to pounce. In my imaginings I crowned her head dragon, in charge of guarding this treasure trove.

When I first reported for work, she had made it quite clear what was expected of me. "You are not to entertain your friends," she said. "When you are here, you work."

"Yes, ma'am," I whispered, looking guilty for no reason at all.

"And above all, be on the lookout for shop-lifters. Watch everybody, even your friends," she went on. "There is an incredible amount of pilfering that takes place in this town every weekend, and a lot of it is done by local high-school students. I don't want it to happen here."

I did my best, but it wasn't easy. By midafternoon the place was packed. Little kids kept wandering around and touching things or asking me dumb questions while I attempted to make change. I just couldn't keep an eye on everything, and I had a nasty suspicion that the head dragon would make me pay for anything that disappeared while I was in charge.

By the time we closed the door at five o'clock, I was exhausted.

"Is it always as busy as this?" I asked.

"This? This was nothing," Mrs. Costello said. "This is off-season. You wait until Christmas or midsummer when the tourists are here."

Then she smiled, the first sign I had that she was human. "I think you did very well for your first day. You stayed calm and dealt with all those annoying questions very efficiently."

"Thank you," I said, amazed at this unexpected praise.

The next day I discovered by accident that looks can be deceiving. We had another busy afternoon, and after we closed the store, we had to spend some time getting everything back in its proper place. I started on the stuffed toys in the corner, which were in complete chaos. In the middle of the group was a dwarf I had fallen in love with. He was fat with deep black eyes and pudgy red cheeks. I had already given him a name, Bumble, and as I rearranged the toys, I put him back in the place of honor.

"There you go, Bumble," I said without thinking. "Sit still like a good dwarf."

"What did you say?" asked the dragon from behind me.

I turned around guiltily. "Oh, I was just talking to that dwarf," I said feeling very stupid.

"Yes, I know," she said impatiently. "But what did you call him?"

"Oh—I called him Bumble. It seemed to suit him."

"Bumble," she said, and her face lit up. "That's perfect! How clever of you! You know, I was searching for the right name for him, but I never could come up with one."

I stared at her in amazement.

"Have you given any of the other toys names?" I asked cautiously.

"Oh, yes," she said, and suddenly she looked like a completely different person, warm and friendly and alive. "Nearly all of them. This fierce-looking dragon is Thunderbringer, and the gentle one over there is Fred—"

"I used to have a dragon named Fred," I blurted out.

After that we had a wonderful time comparing dragons and unicorns and books we had read. It turned out that Mrs. Costello was an ex-schoolteacher who had always had a passion for fantasy and decided to open her store when her husband died.

We talked and talked, and I was in high spirits when I finally got home.

"I was wondering if something had happened to you," my grandmother said as I came in the door.

"It's only just after six, isn't it?" I asked.

"Six? It's seven-thirty!" she said. "Did you meet some friends on the way home?"

"Not exactly," I said. "But I did make a friend."

It was wonderful to have the store to look forward to on weekends. I loved working with all the miniature things. It was like being in another world. And I liked meeting people and talking to Mrs. Costello. I'd been alone for so long that I craved all the bustle and chatter. I really felt a part of something. Now, it was true, I did have a grandmother who took good care of me, baked me cookies, and asked me about school over the dinner table. My grandmother was calm and comforting, but there was still a barrier between us. I just couldn't bring myself to confide in her, and all those years alone had made her very independent, too. She was very wrapped up in her own little world—a world of chickens and tomatoes and the church harvest festival and bingo on Thursday nights, and I never knew if she resented a granddaughter coming into her world.

During the week at school, I still hung around with Raven and her gang. They were always friendly to me, but I could never shake off the feeling of being an outsider. In no way was I really "just one of the kids." There was something—I couldn't describe what—that came between me and the rest of them. Maybe it was all the little things, like the fact that they all smoked and I didn't. Maybe it was that they didn't include me in their evenings. Maybe it was that they were all going together, all twosomes, and I was always the odd one out. Or maybe things could never be the same now that they had made a fool out of me and I had stood up to them.

But I still hung around with them, basically because I had nowhere else to go. Sometimes I had the feeling Mike could have been a good friend if only I'd give him the chance. After all, he had rescued me from the marching band fiasco, and he had kept an eye on me at school. But now, after that stupid letter, I couldn't face him. I wanted badly to apologize to him, but I just couldn't do it. I was too embarrassed and ashamed. When I passed him in the halls, I couldn't even speak properly. Mike seemed to have changed, too. He no longer teased Shannon and me in band practice. He seemed quieter, as if the incident had made him shy, but that was hard to imagine. Mike Gibson and shyness just didn't go together. I suppose he was just hurt.

Of course, another reason—and a very good one—for sticking to Raven and the rest of them was Brad. It gave me an excuse to see him nearly every day. And some days I was quite hopeful about him. It almost seemed as if he did like me. At any rate he noticed me.

"How's my little Lisa?" he would say, putting an arm around me, which usually made Raven tease him or me or both of us. But I put up with the teasing willingly, just to feel that wonderful, strong arm around my shoulder.

Brad's schedule had changed, so now we had a couple of classes together. Sometimes he smiled at me from across the room. Every time I finally began to feel realistic about my chances with Brad, he'd feed me some little crumbs of hope, and I'd be soaring three feet above the ground again. And when I'd make a resolution to pay attention in class, Brad would smile at me, and I'd forget all about the resolution and dream about Brad, only to wake up to hear the teacher asking, "Are you with us, Lisa Daniels?" As usual I wasn't. And my grades were beginning to show it. I realized my daydreaming was worse than ever and getting me in more and more trouble.

But back to Brad. I couldn't help thinking about him! One of the things that gave me a crumb of hope was that Raven was so mean to him. She bullied him and yelled at him, usually in front of the entire group of kids.

"Don't tell me you've got practice again this afternoon," she would snap. "When do I ever get to see you?"

"Oh, come on," Brad said once. "Can't you be a little more understanding? My football is important to me. Doesn't *anybody* understand that?" He appealed to the rest of us.

"I understand," I said softly.

"Oh, *you* would," Raven said, eyeing me poisonously.

Perhaps he really will get tired of her nagging one day, I'd think, full of hope. Then I'd remind myself that if Brad and I got together, I'd have Raven as an enemy—and that would definitely be one step more dangerous than having Raven as a friend. But sometimes I thought I'd do anything, *anything*, for a chance to be with Brad!

Chapter Thirteen

As I said, I was keeping clear of Mike. If I caught sight of him at school, I walked in the other direction—fast. When we had the same class I was a model student and either looked at the teacher—if I wasn't daydreaming—or stared down at my book through the whole period. If there had ever been a time to apologize to him, it was long gone. I had avoided him for too long.

Let's face it, I said to myself. There is something about that boy. Whenever he's near, something terrible happens. I stopped and thought about that one for a minute. Or is it that whenever I've let my daydreaming get me in trouble, he shows up? There was a difference, of course, but it was like trying to decide between the chicken and the egg. In any case, Mike and trouble seemed to go hand in hand.

On Thursday nights Herbie usually came over to take my grandmother to play bingo at the church. Grandma was always concerned about leaving me at home alone, not because she didn't trust me, but because she felt she was deserting me.

"Now, are you sure you'll be all right, Lisa? I'll give you the phone number of the church. Remember to lock the doors. I think there's a good movie on tonight."

She was also very concerned about her appearance. "Does my hair look OK?" she'd ask. "I really must get it cut sometime, but the prices they charge these days . . ." She ran around clucking like an old hen.

That was when I realized how important Herbie was to her, and I wondered what I would do if she ever decided to get married and move in with him. Would I have to go somewhere else? I tried to tell myself they had known each other all these years, and if she were going to marry him, she would have done so long before. But it didn't make me feel much better. Grandma and I had settled into a nice, comfortable life together, and I wanted it to stay that way for a while. I liked her company and all the attention she gave me. I liked her spirit and the way she sometimes acted more like a teenager than a grandmother. And I liked how she was so interested in me. She had already called a conference with all my teachers, just to make sure I was doing OK. I tried to do little things for her in return, like leaving a vase of flowers on her bureau or surprising her with a special dinner, and she appreciated everything so much! I hoped she liked having me around as much as I liked having her around. I was pretty sure she did.

On one Thursday when Herbie arrived, he

boomed from the front door, "Oh, Edith, don't forget your umbrella. Looks like a storm's coming."

"Oh, dear," my grandmother said, fishing for her umbrella in the hall closet. "I still have all the windows open. Lisa, would you run and shut them for me before it starts to rain?"

"Sure," I said. "Have a good time."

I heard their feet scrunch down the driveway and the coughing and spluttering of Herbie's old car as he started it. I went around the house closing windows. From the windows at the back of the house, the view was of a calm fall evening with a clear sky above the dusky hills. But from Grandma's bedroom in the front, I could see a hard bank of black clouds.

I went downstairs, checked the back door to make sure it was locked, and started my homework in front of the TV set. That was something Grandma frowned on, but I enjoyed it. The crackle in the middle of the movie made me jump. I heard the clap of thunder above the fake laughter on the TV. When I went to the window and looked out, it was already raining and quite dark. However, I'm not the sort of person who is particularly scared of storms, so I went back to my French irregular verbs.

By nine o'clock the sound of rain on the porch roof had changed from a soft patter to a hard drumming, but the thunder and lightning hadn't come any closer. I finished my French. The movie ended and another began. A prowler

103

was scaring lonely women, not the sort of thing someone alone in a large house would want to watch. So I flicked through the other channels. It was when I got to a bicycle commercial that I remembered—I had left my bicycle outside!

My grandmother had gone to a great deal of trouble to find me an upright boneshaker with balloon tires. It was old, but it had cost more than Grandma had intended to spend. So I was taking good care of it. Now it was sitting on the grass in the pouring rain and would be the first thing she noticed when she came home.

I grabbed a jacket, held it over my head, and made a dash for the bike. I was wheeling it toward the house when suddenly the wind sprang up and the rain seemed to be blowing from all directions at once. I grabbed at my jacket as it blew from my head, grabbed at the bike as it threatened to fall over, and had just gotten my act together again when I looked up to see the front door slam shut.

"Oh," I said and groaned. "I hope I'm not locked out." I tried the door. I was locked out. There was no point in going around to the back. I had checked the lock on that door.

Terrific, I said to myself.

I had no idea what time bingo finished, but I knew Grandma and Herbie usually got home fairly late. The thought of spending the next two hours on a rainswept porch in a thunderstorm was not very appealing.

I could always go over to the Gibsons', I

thought, then immediately dismissed the idea. I didn't want to face Mike in another one of my crises.

I was determined to find a dry spot. There must be something somewhere, I thought. The garage, maybe. Anywhere but the Gibsons'. The garage was also locked. There was no dry spot on the back porch or the front porch. The wind was blowing across the house, sweeping down both porches and hurling rain at the windows.

OK, I thought. I'll just sit out here shivering in the storm. They'll find my frozen body eventually.

I squatted down miserably under a big grapevine. It did keep the most stinging sort of rain off me, but it dripped big, fat blobs onto my neck.

Be brave, Lisa, I said to myself. You will not give in and go to the Gibsons'. You will stay here or perish in the attempt!

Almost as soon as these words passed through my mind, a blinding flash lit the whole night sky with blue fire and was answered immediately by a terrifying clash of thunder right above me.

"OK. I get the message," I said out loud, springing to my feet and shrinking back next to the side of the house. "I'll go to the Gibsons'. Grandmother would want me to do that."

I splashed through the puddles to their house, and Mike himself opened the door.

"Hi," I said, feeling stupid as usual.

"OK," he said. "What was it this time? A hippopotamus sat in your bathtub? The washing machine went berserk?"

"Mike," I said, "I went out in the storm to bring my bike in. The wind blew the door shut. Now I'm locked out. I'm sorry."

Mike smiled and sighed. "Did you know life was quite peaceful until you moved in next door? I got up, went to school, watched TV. Nothing ever happened."

"I said I was sorry."

"Oh, don't be. Peaceful can be boring, you know. Now my life is quite exciting. I wake up and wonder what crazy thing you'll do today."

"That's not fair. Ninety-nine percent of my life is spent doing sane, normal things. You just happen to see that other one percent."

"Why me? That's what I ask myself."

"Believe me, it's not intentional. I ask myself the same question every day. I don't particularly enjoy having someone grinning over each of my misfortunes."

"I don't grin," Mike said, grinning as he said it. "I suppose you want to come in?"

I was still dripping in his doorway.

"That was the general idea," I said.

"Well, I don't know," Mike said, looking serious. "I'm home all alone. My parents are off playing bingo. I don't think they'd approve of me letting in strange girls."

"That's OK," I said stiffly. "I'll just go back to my porch and freeze." I turned away.

106

"Don't be a dope," he said, grabbing my arm and pulling me roughly into the house. "Of course you can come in. In fact, you must be sent from heaven. You take French, right? I was just stuck in the middle of my French homework, and I was about to phone someone for help."

I stood in the front hall while my numb fingers tried to peel off my dripping jacket. My pant legs were dripping too, and little puddles were forming around my feet.

"I hope your parents won't mind," I said.

"They'll be furious," Mike said, trying to look serious again, but this time not succeeding. "But I'll risk it, if only for the sake of getting some help with French." Then he looked at me standing there forlornly like a half-drowned kitten, and he smiled. "You better come into the kitchen where it's warm." He turned to lead the way.

"Excuse the mess," he said as we went through the big family room. It really was a mess, full of old, mismatched furniture, tables littered with schoolbooks, newspapers, sewing, but it looked like a room a family lived in. I couldn't help feeling envious that I had never known a room like that.

It took us ages to do Mike's homework. Neither of us was too gifted in French, and Mike had a different teacher than I had, so we had different assignments. But we struggled so hard over it, we didn't have time to remember we were Mike and Lisa. Finally, Mike closed the book in triumph.

"There. All done," he said. "Thanks a million, Lisa. I'd never have managed to finish that on my own."

"I don't know that I was much help," I said.

"Sure you were. Two heads are always better than one."

"I wonder if my grandmother's home yet," I said uncertainly.

"I'll phone, if you like," Mike said. He got up and went across the room to the phone. After a minute he shook his head. "Nobody there yet. I bet they're having a great old time, living it up at bingo. Hey, I'm starving. Are you? Why don't we fix ourselves a snack?"

"Sure," I said and watched in amazement as Mike emptied the contents of the fridge onto the kitchen table. Then he piled everything one by one onto two slices of bread. "There," he said, giving me his famous grin. "That's what I call a sandwich—bologna, Swiss cheese, salami, dill pickles, lettuce, tomato, mayonnaise, and sprouts. Have I forgotten anything?"

"The kitchen sink?" I asked.

Mike slapped his hand to his forehead, jumped up, and made a move for the sink.

"Do you ever stop clowning around?" I asked him as he sat down again.

"Sure," he said, "when I'm at ease with somebody."

"And you're not at ease with me?"

108

"Well, you must admit we've had our differences."

"I'll make a great effort to behave normally from now on, if you'll make an effort to stop teasing me."

He smiled. "OK. You know, we've never talked like two ordinary people. I really don't know much about you. Tell me about those famous parents of yours."

So I told him. He was a good listener. He didn't make any of his normal wisecracks, and I found myself telling him more than I had intended.

"That's a bummer," he said when I got to the part about both of them being too busy for me. "I don't know what I'd do if neither of my parents had time for me."

"Well, of course they really *want* to have me with them," I said, defending them. "Once Mama's career gets going again, everything will be all right. This stay with Grandma is only temporary. Mama says I can go back to her as soon as she's settled down again. And that can't be too long."

"Sure," Mike said, not looking up from his sandwich.

"And then Raven will want to come and visit me and meet all the Hollywood stars she pretends not to care about," I said jokingly.

Mike played with his sandwich. Finally, he cleared his throat. "Lisa, there's something I've been meaning to say to you."

"What?"

"I thought Raven would have dropped you before this, and I wouldn't have to say it. But now it looks as though you're going to be included permanently. I just wanted to warn you, because I like you and care what happens to you. I don't think they're the right friends for you."

"Why?" I whispered, knowing the answer.

"Because you're not like them. They do different things. They have a different set of values from you and different ideas of having fun."

"Mike," I said, half-annoyed, half-flattered, "I can take care of myself. I'm not a complete baby. I've got a pretty good idea about what Raven and her friends do for fun. But that doesn't mean I go along with it. I just see them at school because I need someone to talk to. After all, I have to have *some* friends in this world!"

"You have me," he said simply.

"Oh, yeah," I said bitterly. "To haul me out of trouble and tease me."

Mike reached out his hand, and his fingers closed around mine. "Lisa," he said, "I really do care about you. In fact—"

Suddenly I realized we were sitting pretty close together. Mike's eyes were very bright as he looked at me. His face came closer to mine. Then I knew, with something close to amazement, that he was going to kiss me. And then, with honest amazement, I knew I didn't want to move away.

At that moment the front door opened, and someone yelled, "Hi, Mike! We're home!"

We moved apart hastily and were sitting in positions of complete innocence by the time the Gibsons came through to the kitchen.

"Oh, Mike," his mother said. "I see you have a visitor. How nice."

"And what have you two been up to?" his father teased. I felt myself blushing as if I were guilty.

What, I wondered, would have happened if his parents hadn't shown up then?

Chapter Fourteen

The next Sunday Raven and Dorette paid me a visit at the store. We had just gotten in a new shipment of turquoise Indian jewelry, and Mrs. Costello had me writing price tags for the pieces between customers.

"These are beautiful things," I said. "I've never seen anything like them."

Mrs. Costello looked at them fondly. "Yes, you don't see this quality too often. I get mine straight from a Hopi Indian supplier in Arizona. I'm the only person who stocks it for miles around. People even come from San Francisco to buy from me."

I particularly admired one bracelet. It looked like a rainbow made of natural stones, bands of turquoise and pink coral and other stones I didn't recognize. I put it on a bed of black velvet and placed it in front of me where I could gaze at it.

Raven and Dorette noticed the jewelry immediately when they arrived.

"Nice stuff you've got here," Dorette said, looking around and nodding. "I like the turquoise."

Raven came over to join her. "Hey, look, that's pretty," she said, picking up my bracelet. She turned it over. "But look at the price!"

"We cater to tourists, remember," I said. "You can charge tourists what you like."

"Hey, Dorette," Raven said, slipping on the bracelet. "It goes well with this sweater, doesn't it?"

"Why don't you ask Brad to buy it for your birthday?" Dorette said.

Again I felt a pang of jealousy I had no right to feel. Why should he be so much in love with Raven when she treated him so badly? If only I were her.

I saw Brad arriving at *my* birthday party, giving me his wonderful smile and saying, "A little bird told me you wanted this." He would slip the turquoise bracelet onto my wrist while I smiled up at him. Then he would take me in his arms. . . .

"Lisa!" I heard Mrs. Costello's voice call from the back of the store. "Wake up, dear. I think these people are waiting to be helped."

"Coming, Mrs. Costello," I called and snapped myself back from Brad's arms. "You guys better go," I said to Raven and Dorette. "My boss gets mad if I stand around and talk."

"All right, we can take a hint. We're going," they said, laughing. They giggled their way out of the store.

The afternoon was a busy one. It was one of those beautiful, clear fall days that arrives right after a storm. The sky was an inverted blue glass bowl, and the trees were tinted red and gold. The tourists came out from San Francisco and Oakland, and there wasn't a parking space anywhere in the square.

It was only when we were ready to close up that I noticed the rainbow bracelet was missing. My stomach took a dive. How could it have disappeared? We hadn't sold it, and I had been there all the time. I hadn't turned my back. Sure, I may have indulged in one or two little daydreams, but it was right in front of my cash register. I searched the floor to see if it had been knocked down by mistake, but it hadn't.

Of course, the thought of Raven did cross my mind. She had been awfully interested in the bracelet. But that was impossible. I had been watching her all the time—hadn't I? Raven had examined the bracelet and asked the price. Then she had put it back again—I thought. Raven wouldn't—not to her own friend!

I couldn't take any chances. When Mrs. Costello paid me, I took a deep breath. "I'm going to put my thirty dollars straight back into the till for one of those Indian bracelets," I said. "I've had my eye on it all afternoon."

"Oh, you don't have to pay thirty for it," Mrs. Costello said. "I'll let you have it at cost. Which one was it?"

For one terrible moment I thought she would call on me to produce it. "The rainbow one," I said. "I just wrapped it to give to a friend."

114

"Lucky friend," Mrs. Costello said. "I'll only charge you fifteen. That's what I paid wholesale."

Well, fifteen dollars wasn't as bad as thirty. I paid up and left. But I still worried about it. The worst thing was not knowing. Part of me felt just terrible for suspecting my friend. I could never come right out and ask Raven if she took it. What would she think of me if I was wrong? And if I was right, she would never admit it. I guessed I'd never know for whom I had spent fifteen of my precious dollars.

But on Monday morning I did. I was sitting opposite Raven in history when I looked up and there was the bracelet, right there on her wrist. I was so shocked I knocked my notebook off my desk. It crashed to the floor, scattering papers. The teacher frowned, and several kids snickered.

"Here, let me help you," Raven said, joining me on the floor to pick up the papers, flaunting the bracelet. I had to admit she was cool. I also knew I had to pluck up enough courage to ask her about it.

I nabbed her as soon as the bell rang. "Hey, let me see that bracelet," I said. "Where did you get it?"

"Oh, this?" Raven said, her face relaxed and serene. "Isn't it pretty? I bought it this weekend."

"At our store?" I asked. "I know you liked it, but I thought you said it was too expensive. I didn't notice you come back and buy it."

"Oh, I didn't get it at your store," Raven said, gathering up her things and beginning to walk away. "Those were stupid prices. I have a friend who can give me much better deals than those. I went to him instead. Wasn't it lucky he had the same one?"

I longed to say, "You're lying. Mrs. Costello said she was the only person for miles around to stock this Indian jewelry." But the words wouldn't come out.

Coward, I said to myself as Raven walked off. But it wasn't any good. I still couldn't make myself confront her. After all, there *was* a tiny shadow of doubt. How could she seem so relaxed and friendly if she was lying? Was it possible she really did know someone who got her the bracelet? Raven knew a lot of people, so I couldn't be one hundred percent sure. But I was sure enough to know that I couldn't stay friendly with Raven anymore.

When I got home, Herbie was there again. He seemed to be coming more and more often. He and Grandma were on the porch, sipping iced tea.

"Well, it's my favorite little lady," Herbie said cheerfully. "How was school today? Did you learn anything?"

I smiled at him. "I learned one thing the hard way. Not to trust people so easily."

"Quite right. Never trust anybody," he said. "And who was the person you learned not to trust?"

"Someone I thought was my friend. A girl named Raven Delgado."

"Delgado?" he said. "That name rings a bell. That was the woman who had the wild daughter."

"That sounds like Raven," I said.

"I remember her mother complaining about her. Always wild, she was, right from the start. But I wonder if this Raven is any relative? What sort of name is Raven anyway?"

"A ridiculous one," supplied Grandma.

"Raven must be the daughter," I said. "The wild one."

Herbie shook his head. "There was only the one daughter, and her name was Alice."

Alice, ha! It must be a well-guarded secret.

I ran upstairs jubilantly. Alice Delgado! Somehow now that I knew her real name wasn't Raven, I felt much better. I was pretty sure she wouldn't want her real name leaked all over school. I wondered how many kids knew it. It gave me a feeling of power over her for the first time. Try any more funny business with me, Alice Delgado, I thought, and I'll tell the whole world your name!

Chapter Fifteen

By now I was positive I didn't want Raven for a friend. But I worried about how to move away from her group without making too many waves. I was smart enough to know that Raven would be the worst sort of enemy to have in school. She knew everybody, she was popular, and she was also, as I had seen, quite ruthless.

Then things sorted themselves out for me— though not exactly in the way I would have chosen. It all started one lunchtime when Brad hadn't shown up again.

"Where's Brad?" Dorette asked innocently, looking around.

"How should I know?" Raven snapped. "You don't think he tells me where he's going these days!"

"He had to see the coach again," Rusty explained. "About a tour of the UC campus."

"I never thought I'd lose my boyfriend to a football coach," Raven whined.

"You can quit griping, Raven. He's coming now," Kathy said. My heart gave its usual stupid leap as I saw Brad strolling across the field toward us, hands in the pockets of his letter jacket, looking relaxed and smiling. Why did he have to be *so* gorgeous, so right for me, and so much in love with Raven?

"Well, how nice of you to grace us with your presence," Raven said, her voice smooth as honey but her eyes flashing black fire. "And how kind of your coach to let you out of his sight for a few minutes."

"Couldn't do without me again, huh?" he said, grinning. "Well, I do have that effect on some girls."

I knew it was dangerous to tease Raven in her present mood; she looked furious.

"Did you get the tour set up?" Rusty asked, trying to relieve the tension.

"Oh, yeah," Brad said, his face lighting up. "They want me to come this weekend. For the whole weekend! Imagine that. I get the full celebrity treatment. Isn't that great?"

"Where are you going this weekend?" Raven asked sharply.

"UC—Berkeley. I told you about it. They're probably going to offer me a scholarship, and they want me to come down to the campus this weekend."

Brad looked so excited. He couldn't stop smiling.

But Raven's mouth was set in a hard line. "And what about Jamie's party?" she asked icily. "I thought we were going to that."

"Oh, Jamie's party," Brad said, and his face

fell. "Well, I'm sorry, I guess we'll just have to miss it."

"But I wanted to go. Am I going to have to spend my whole life playing second fiddle to a lousy football?"

"Raven, be reasonable," Brad pleaded. "I can't turn down the chance to see UC just so you can go to a party."

"But I was looking forward to it," she said.

Brad looked so hurt, so vulnerable, that I spoke before I could stop myself. "Come on, Raven," I said. "People have to put their careers before parties. You know that. And you know how much football means to Brad. He needs you to back him up."

Before I'd finished speaking, I knew it was a mistake. Raven's eyes flashed at me.

"How would you know?" she asked. "You've never even had a boyfriend. All you can do is gaze longingly at other girls' guys." I started to protest. "Oh, don't think I haven't noticed the way you stare at Brad with those big eyes of yours," she interrupted. "I used to think it was funny. Now it makes me sick."

Brad came over to me and put an arm around me protectively. "Enough, Raven. Lisa hasn't done anything to you. As for me, maybe I've had about all I can take." He stalked off.

"In that case," Raven shouted after him, "I might just get someone else to take me to the party Saturday night. And let me tell you, there are plenty of guys standing in line for me!"

120

Brad didn't answer, so Raven gathered herself together and walked away, leaving the rest of us standing in silence. For one wild moment I had hoped Brad wanted me instead of Raven. But he had been too angry for me to tell. However, he *had* draped his arm around me when he yelled at Raven. What did that mean? I knew Raven was wondering, too.

Things were pretty tense the rest of the day, and I stayed out of Raven's way. I hadn't forgotten the look she'd given me. If looks could kill, I would be lying in a coffin. So I was surprised to hear her calling my name after school. She rushed up to me with Dorette and flashed me a smile. "Look, Lisa. About lunchtime. Let's forget it. I was in a bad mood."

"OK," I said uneasily, wondering if my mother and the lure of Hollywood still had a hold over her. I didn't really think Raven would feel bad about hurting someone else's feelings.

"Dorette and I are going shopping. Want to come?" she asked.

I was about to say no, but decided it might be wise to go. After all, it was easiest when you went along with Raven and what she wanted.

We walked across the square to the small department store, Grainger's, on the side street. Raven decided to try on bikinis, Dorette looked at hair ornaments, and I tried to be neither too friendly nor too hostile. At last Dorette bought some hair ribbons. But Raven didn't like any of the bikinis. "There's nothing I want here," Raven said. "This store is so behind the times." She started to walk out. "Besides," she added, "I've got a pile of homework tonight. This book bag weighs a ton. Here, Lisa, take my purse, will you? My right arm is nearly breaking."

I took her purse and slung it over my shoulder. Then we left. We were still standing blinking in the strong sunlight when I felt someone tap me on the shoulder.

"Just a minute, young ladies."

I turned around to see two men standing behind us, one old and bald, the other young and muscular. I thought they were muggers. "What do you want?" I asked and heard my voice tremble.

"To see your bags. We think you've been shoplifting," they said.

I smiled in relief. "Oh, I thought you were going to rob us. You scared me for a minute."

"Do you mind if we search your belongings?" one of the men said.

"No," I said, hoping no one we knew would come by. The older man took my book bag, and the other took Raven's purse.

"I'll say this, you're a pretty cool customer," the young one said. He opened Raven's purse and held up a black bikini. I looked across at Raven, waiting for her to say something. She didn't.

"But that's not my purse," I stammered.

"Oh? Whose is it, then?"

I hated to accuse someone else, but I wasn't going to be caught for something I didn't do. "It's hers," I said, pointing to Raven.

"Is this yours, miss?" the old man asked.

Raven nodded and looked suitably serious and worried. "Yes, it is. But, you see, I couldn't carry it because I have so many books today. Lisa's had it on her shoulder all afternoon. I had no idea she would try and use my purse for something like this."

I looked across at Dorette. Wouldn't she defend me? But Dorette also shook her head and said, "Lisa, how could you do that to Raven?"

I felt fear prickle my spine. I wanted to shake somebody, to yell, "They're lying. It's a trick. Raven's paying me back for today!"

"Let's go inside, all of you," the old man said. He led us into his office, a dark, windowless little room like a prison. I felt so scared I thought I might throw up. A woman came in and searched us all. Raven and Dorette, of course, had nothing on them. Why would they, since I was carrying the stolen item for them?

"You two can go," she said.

"Now, young lady," the big, bald-headed man said, turning to me. "How can we get in touch with your parents? We like parents to be present before we call the police."

I had a wild desire to laugh. What would they say if I told them my mom was a famous movie star and my dad was Jack Daniels, NBC correspondent in Egypt? Somehow I didn't think they'd believe me. Instead I said, "I live with my grandmother."

When I told them her name and gave them the phone number, the old man said he knew her. "We go to the same church," he said. "She's going to be pretty upset when she finds out what you've done."

While we waited for Grandma to come, I felt sick with worry. What would she say? Would she believe me? She was on my side, wasn't she?

The bald-headed man phoned the police and found I had no previous criminal record, which was one good thing. In between being scared and worried, I thought about Raven. I remembered how smoothly she had taken the bracelet. She must do that sort of thing pretty often. Today she couldn't lose either way. If I hadn't been caught, she'd have gotten her bikini. Since I had been caught, she had taught me not to interfere with her and Brad. I'd always known she was a person to be reckoned with. I just hadn't realized how much.

Grandma arrived, bulldozing in like an army tank.

I ran to her. "Grandma," I cried, "I swear—"

She didn't say anything, but took my hand in hers and faced the old man. "Howard," she said, frowning at him, "what's this I hear about my granddaughter shoplifting?"

"We found a bikini in her purse," Howard

said. "She had just taken it out of the store."

Grandma turned to me. "Lisa?" she asked.

"Grandma, I didn't take it. It's not even my purse. It's Raven's. She asked me to carry it out of the store. The bikini was in it, but I had no idea—"

"Which girl was this?" Grandma cut in.

"Raven Delgado."

"Ha!" said my grandmother. "That explains it. Well, Howard, if Lisa said she didn't do it, that's good enough for me."

I stared at her, relieved. She took my word!

Howard looked worried, as if torn between wanting to believe my grandmother and not wanting to believe me.

Grandma picked up the bikini and examined it. "She was supposed to have stolen *this*?" she asked incredulously.

Howard nodded.

"What size are you, Lisa?" she asked.

"About a five."

"Ha!" said Grandma again. "There you are then, Howard. That proves it. Why would anyone who is a size five steal a size eight bikini? Come on, Lisa. We're going home." She marched me out of the office.

All over me was a wonderful warm glow. My grandmother cares, I thought.

When we got home, Herbie was there, sitting in the kitchen. Apparently my little adventure had interrupted one of his visits.

Grandma told him the story, and he snorted

indignantly. He was all for confronting Raven's family with the incident. "A thing like that shouldn't go unpunished. That girl's got a few things to learn about wrong and right. If I were you, Edith, I'd get on the phone with the Delgados right now."

I perched on the very edge of the kitchen chair, waiting anxiously for Grandma's answer. Please don't do it, I begged silently. I wasn't going to hang around with Raven or her friends ever, ever again. And Howard must be suspicious now. Raven would be watched very carefully the next time she set foot in Grainger's. Let's just leave her alone.

"Now, Herbie, I don't think that's necessary. Do you, Lisa?"

I breathed a huge sigh of relief. "No, not at all. I promise I'll never have anything to do with Raven again. I learned my lesson."

"Just make sure you keep that promise," said Grandma a bit more sternly than usual.

"Yes, ma'am," I said.

"How did you wind up with friends like Raven in the first place?" she asked.

"Oh, Grandma, you know. Some people aren't what they seem to be. And others are like chameleons, changing their personalities to suit the people they're with. Raven's a little of both. Besides, she was one of the first girls at school who wanted to make friends."

"I understand," she said quietly.

"Oh, Grandma," I cried suddenly, getting

126

up and hugging her. "I'm so glad you believed me. I was afraid—"

"That's OK, dear." She patted me on the back.

I pulled away from her and looked over at Herbie to see him smiling fondly at both of us.

Chapter Sixteen

On the way to school the next day, I worried a lot about what I would do when I saw Raven. Of course, I would have liked to have been very brave, to have gone right up to her and told her what I thought of her in front of her whole crowd. But I didn't think that would be very smart. For one thing, I was still the new girl; and for another, I had seen enough of how she managed to swing people to her side whenever she wanted. I would probably come off the loser with more enemies than I had bargained for. And with the number of friends I had, I certainly didn't need more enemies.

As it turned out, I didn't have to worry about Raven. She ignored me totally, passing me in the hall as if I no longer existed. It was probably just as well. She was hardly worth a confrontation. A clean break was much easier. I was eating lunch alone when Mike found me.

"Where's the ever-present Raven?" he asked.

"As far away as possible, I hope," I said.

"Oh?" He raised an eyebrow. "So you finally found out for yourself, did you?"

"Yeah. Did you hear?"

He sat down beside me. "A few rumors. A lot of kids have heard them, but since Raven's spreading them, no one's paying much attention. No one but her crowd puts much stock in anything she says. So, don't worry. In a day or two everyone will have forgotten. You won't have a reputation or anything. In a way, I'm glad it happened. You're better off without them. They weren't the friends for you, Lisa. In fact, I was scared you'd get into some kind of trouble with them. Something a lot worse than this, I mean."

"Since I'm pretty good at getting into trouble on my own?" I asked.

He grinned at me, a warm, friendly grin that made me feel as good as Grandma's loving defense of me the day before.

"Mike," I said, "I want to thank you for trying to warn me. I'm sorry I was rude."

"It's OK," he said, looking a bit embarrassed. But then the old Mike was back. "Hey, look at it this way. From now on you can have lunch with someone witty, sophisticated, and good-looking."

"No kidding. Who?" I asked.

At that moment it felt as if a great load had been lifted from my shoulders. I was free of Raven and all her phony friends. Then it hit me—no more Raven meant no more Brad. Could I survive without seeing Brad at lunch every day? Well, I'd just have to, somehow.

When I started having lunch with Mike, I wondered why on earth I had stuck with Raven for so long. The only thing she and her entourage liked to talk about was themselves—petty conversations of people trying to score points against other people. With Mike I could really talk. I found myself telling him how disappointed I was that my parents hadn't even written.

"And it wouldn't hurt my mother to phone once in a while," I said. "After all, it's not as if she were on the other side of the world. It doesn't cost *that* much to phone from Los Angeles. Of course, I know she's been really busy this year, and that as soon as she gets a moment—"

"Lisa," Mike cut in. "Maybe you should stop hoping. Some people aren't cut out to be mothers."

"I know," I said. "But I *can't* stop hoping. She's my *mother*."

It's funny that Mike and I should have had that conversation that day because that same evening Mama called. Right in the middle of dinner.

"Now who can that be?" my grandmother asked, looking annoyed. "It doesn't seem to matter what time I put a hot meal on the table, someone always interrupts it."

"I'll get it," I said, jumping up from the table.

"Hello? Is Lisa there, please?" said a voice I didn't recognize.

"This is Lisa."

"Lisa?" The squeal at the other end nearly

130

shattered my eardrums. "It's Mama, honey. Lisa, baby, how have you been? I've been so worried about you."

"I'm just fine, Mama," I said. Somehow I couldn't match her enthusiasm.

"You sound so grown up," my mother said. "It must be months since I saw you last."

"Over a year," I said.

"As long as that? My, doesn't time fly. Baby, if only you knew how I missed you, but you see I couldn't go on living with your father. He didn't seem to think my career mattered at all. But it was obvious he could provide a better home for you than I. He wasn't always flitting around the country. I thought he had his nice regular job and the apartment. I was horrified to hear he'd just upped and left you. What kind of man would do that to his child?"

"He has to follow his career, Mama," I said. "Just like you."

There was a moment's pause on the other end before she went on, bubbly as ever. "But, darling, I just had to call you to tell you my wonderful news. The divorce from your father finally came through."

"That's wonderful news?" I asked. I couldn't think of much worse. Now there was no hope of us ever being a family again.

"Well, it is to me, darling. You see, I've met this wonderful man—and now we can get married."

She stopped, waiting for me to say some-

131

thing. I opened my mouth, but nothing would come out.

"Lisa? Are you still there? Lisa, say something. Say you're pleased for me."

How could I talk when I was hurtling down an elevator shaft into nothingness? Mama had left me; Dad had left me; and now Mama was replacing Dad with some stranger.

"How can I say I'm pleased?" I said, trying to keep my voice from trembling, "when I've never even met him? I don't even know his name."

"It's Mort, darling. Mort Sylvester. He's my new agent."

Mort, I thought. As in mortician, mortuary, and mortifying—hardly the most promising name for a future stepfather.

"Well, when are you getting married?" I made myself ask, trying to sound bright and cheerful. "Do I get a chance to meet him before the wedding?"

"Of course you do. You know I wouldn't marry anyone you couldn't get along with."

"I don't think it matters too much if we get along or not."

"Of course it matters. The moment we get a suitable house, you'll be coming back to live with us."

"Live with you?"

"Certainly. You don't think I'd really abandon my baby, do you? Lisa, you do want to come home, don't you?"

What could I say? I had dreamed of going to live with my mother, had prayed for that day, but now I wasn't sure anymore. Did I really want to live with an unknown man named Mort? And leave Grandma and Herbie and Mike?

"I guess so," I said.

"Of course you do," my mother said. "We'll have such fun being together again. We'll send you to a good private school, and you can do all the things you've always wanted to, and maybe we can all go on a trip to Europe together. Won't that be nice?"

I tried to answer, but I couldn't. She went on. "Lisa, I've missed so much of your growing up, but I do want to be part of it now. You do still love me, don't you?"

"I'll always love you, Mama," I said tiredly.

"And I love you, baby. I better go now. Mort is making signs at me that we're late. But I'll be calling you again very soon. Mort and I will arrange to come up and see you in the next week or so. Maybe we'll fly up to San Francisco for a weekend and pop up to see you then. Anyway it will be very soon, I promise you. I can't wait to see you again."

"I want to see you, too."

"Bye-bye, darling. Be a good girl."

"Bye, Mama."

There was a click at the other end, and I put the phone down slowly.

"And what, in heaven's name, did she want?" my grandmother asked.

133

"She's getting married again," I said, walking back to my chair like a zombie. "And she wants me to go and live with her."

Grandma made a face and said something that sounded a lot like "humph."

I closed that topic of discussion and didn't bring it up again until just before I was going to bed.

"Grandma," I said cautiously, "about Mom."

She sighed. "Oh, honey, I'm sorry. I don't mean to be so grouchy. It's just that your mother has never been very fair to you or your father. She's not reliable. Please, Lisa, don't get your hopes up too high about going home, OK? Try not to think about it too much. If it happens, it happens. But in case it doesn't, keep trying to make a go of it here. All right?"

"Yes," I answered, feeling slightly puzzled.

But if Mama said she'd come for me, then she'd come. Wouldn't she?

Chapter Seventeen

It wasn't until later that it really hit me—I might be going home to Mama, just as I had always dreamed I would. I lay back on my pillow, and drifted into a daydream that for once was probably going to come true. The car would pull up outside the house, just as I happened to be walking home from school with Mike. Mama would leap out almost before the car came to a complete stop.

"There she is, that's my baby," she would shout.

Mike would stand there openmouthed as Mama pushed past him to envelop me in a hug. Then a tall, gray-haired, serious-looking man, with heavy-framed glasses, would climb out of the car to join us.

"Don't tell me this is Lisa," he'd say, and the frown lines would change to smile lines. "I was expecting to see a little girl, but this is a young lady."

Then he'd hug me, too, strong and reassuring as if to say from now on he'd take care of me.

Then Mama would say, "Let's not stick

around here any longer than we have to. Let's get the evening flight back to LA. Are you ready to go, Lisa?"

"But I've got to pack my things," I'd say, and Mama would laugh her high, sweet laugh. "Silly, we'll just leave all your old things behind. That way we can go out and buy new ones together."

Then I'd wave goodbye to Mike and Grandma, and off we'd go, leaving a cloud of white dust hovering behind us on the lane. . . .

End of daydream. I opened my eyes. Why didn't I feel terribly excited or happy? Was it because I had to leave my clothes behind—the clothes I had bought with my hard-earned money? Was it because I didn't get a chance to say a proper goodbye to my grandmother? Was it because I was going to miss her and Mike? Or was it because somehow I didn't believe Mort was going to look like Mr. Suburban American Father?

Well, I might not have been jumping for joy, but I was pleased my mother wanted me back— actually wanted me back! Just wanting me was a step in the right direction.

I couldn't wait to tell Mike in the morning, especially since it would give me a chance to prove him wrong for once!

"I had a phone call last night," I said smugly as soon as I saw him. I had looked for him all morning at school and finally ran into him coming out of the gym.

"Big deal," he said. "Lots of people get phone calls, otherwise Ma Bell would go out of business."

"Very funny. But wait till you hear who this phone call was from." I paused dramatically. "My mother. How about that, after what you said yesterday?"

I looked suitably triumphant. Mike looked surprised.

"No kidding? What did she want?"

"Nothing important. Only to tell me she's getting married again and wants me to live with her."

Mike's eyes flew wide open. "She really said that?"

"Cross my heart and hope to die."

"So when are you going?" He sounded disappointed.

"I don't know for sure. She didn't say. But very soon." It was easy to ignore my grandmother's warning. I wanted my mother so much.

"Oh," he said. He traced patterns in the dirt with his toe. "And do you really want to go?"

"Of course I do. You know I do. It's what I've always dreamed of. Wouldn't you want to live with your own mother?"

"Well, yes," he said slowly. "I suppose so."

We walked together in silence down the path under the old oak trees. Two orange-and-black butterflies danced past us, landed for a second, then flew off again.

"Did you like living with your mother before?" Mike asked suddenly.

"That's a weird question," I said. "Of course I did."

"How long has it been since you lived with her?"

"About a year and a half. But she was gone a lot of the time before that, too. Why are you asking me all this?"

"I don't want you to get your hopes up too high, that's all," he said.

"What do you mean?" I asked, but I knew exactly what he meant. "You don't think she'll really turn up, is that right?" He sounded just like Grandma.

"Oh, she might. Right now she might decide that a daughter around the house would be the perfect thing. But then she might decide you're in the way again and dump you—"

"That's a terrible thing to say!" I shouted.

"Well, it happened before, didn't it? She walked out on you before. Any woman who walks out on her family once can do it again, you know."

Suddenly, without warning, tears flooded my eyes. "Why are you doing this?" I demanded. "Why are you trying to make me feel bad? Why are you spoiling the one spot of happiness in my life?"

Mike stopped and turned toward me. "Oh,

Lisa," he said and put his hands on my shoulders, holding me so he could look into my eyes. "Don't you see? I don't want you to get hurt. I'm just trying to spare you. I've never met your mother, but I picked up a pretty clear picture of her from you, and I don't believe she'll go through with this. You'd be much better off staying here. And think about it. Is this really the only happiness in your life? What about your grandmother? . . . What about me?"

"But you don't understand," I stammered. "All my life I've dreamed of going home where I belong."

"Lisa," he said, "you're a daydreamer. That's just a dream. The way you think things should be. I think you belong here. Your grandmother loves you—and I'd miss you if you went away."

I looked into his face. His blue eyes were searching mine, pleading. "Lisa, I've cared about you ever since you fell over backward into those chickens. I can't tell you how much I'd miss you if you went."

"I'd miss you too, Mike," I said shakily. "You've been like a big brother to me."

"I'd like to be more than a big brother," he said in a strangled voice. He reached out, took hold of my shoulders, and drew me to him. His lips brushed mine. Then he crushed me to him and was kissing me.

I tried to push him away. "Mike," I panted. "Mike, everyone can see us."

"Let them see."

"But, Mike, I don't know if I want this."

He let me go then, his arms dropping to his sides. "You don't care about me?" he asked. His voice cracked, and I felt mean and wretched.

"No—yes, I do," I stammered. "Oh, I don't know what I feel. I do care about you, Mike. Really. It's made all the difference, knowing you here. But I'm so confused right now. I'm going to be leaving soon. I don't think I can handle getting romantically involved with someone and then having to leave him."

"Yeah, I understand," he said, turning away so I couldn't see his face. "I guess it was stupid of me, when you're just about to leave."

Had that been another lie? Had I only said that to soften the blow that I didn't want him as my boyfriend? I really didn't know. I had always dreamed I'd know the right boy when he come along, that I'd get goose bumps when he touched me and float when he kissed me. But that didn't seem to happen with Mike and yet . . . I didn't know, I just didn't know. My world seemed to stay stable only for a few minutes before it turned upside-down again. If I wanted Mike only as a brother, how come I felt this awful pang at leaving him?

We turned back toward school.

"You know what?" Mike said, taking my hand. "I was planning to ask you to the homecoming dance, but I guess you won't be here that long. I was wondering—" he said and paused. "You and I ought to have one special

evening together. One we can remember for always. There's a concert on Saturday night at
the town hall. Would you like to go with me?"

"Yes," I said. "If you promise to behave
yourself."

"I can't promise anything," Mike said, giving me his familiar grin, "but I'll try."

Chapter Eighteen

Now that I thought my time in Sonoma was drawing to a close, everything I did became special. I found myself thinking, I'll never do this again, or This may be the last time in my whole life. . . . Grandma did not encourage such thoughts.

Even feeding the chickens, for example. I never thought I'd enjoy that, certainly never thought I'd become attached to a chicken, but I knew them all by name. I always made sure Bonnie—the one with only one eye—got her fair share, that Lulu, the big Rhode Island red, did not push the others out of the way, and that Daisy got complimented on the number of eggs she laid. Now it seemed likely that I'd never feed another chicken in my life. And I knew that I was going to miss them. I was going to miss the way they waited for me, peering expectantly through the wire five minutes before I was due; the way they all followed me devotedly as I walked across their pen with the pail. Now there would be no more pets. No more Jellybean jumping onto my bed in the morning and purring like a buzz saw as he crept up toward my face, or rubbing against my legs when I was sitting at the table, letting me know that he was there, just in case I let a piece of meat fall by accident. Grandma didn't approve of feeding Jellybean from the table, so it had to fall "by accident."

Then there was the store. I was really going to miss that. Not just because of the money—although it made me feel proud when I could stop and buy Grandma a little present on the way home. I knew I was going to miss Mrs. Costello and all the little animals, and she was going to miss me, too. One evening she invited me to dinner at her house.

"You'd better come now, while you can," she said. "I don't want to find that that mother of yours has turned up overnight and whisked you off, and we haven't even had a chance to say goodbye."

"I wouldn't leave without saying goodbye to you," I said, but I remembered that in my day-dream that was just what I had done.

After dinner Mrs. Costello showed me all her treasures, from stuffed elephants to large uncut opals. Then she handed me a package.

"I've worked with a lot of girls in my time," she said, "and most of them were on a different planet from me. But not you. If I'd ever had a daughter, I'd have wanted her to be a lot like you. Keep in touch, OK?" Then I opened the package, and it was Bumble.

I couldn't find any words to say. I just hugged her.

No more working in stores, I thought afterward. Mama would never let her daughter take a job. And no more football games.

But that made that next Friday night's game very special. This may be the very last football game I ever play at, I thought. If my mother sent me to an exclusive private school, as she had mentioned, there certainly wouldn't be a football team.

Anyway, that football game took on a magic quality for me, and everything seemed to go just right. My hair curled softly after I washed it; the first pair of pantyhose I took out of the drawer had no runs in it; and when I sat next to Shannon in the band room and began to put on my eye makeup, my eyes seemed extra bright and sparkling.

Shannon noticed it, too. "Gee, you look pretty tonight," she said. "Are you going on a special date afterward or something?"

"I wish," I said, and remembered about Mike. Mike would take me on a special date any time, but somehow I couldn't picture a special date with him. He was not my Mr. Right; he was just good old Mike who was around when I needed him. When he kissed me, I didn't hear bells or sirens or get goose bumps. I knew all those things would happen as soon as I met the right boy. And I knew who the right boy was, if only he'd ever see it!

We finished dressing and went out to join the rest of the band. I had had another month to practice, so I wasn't worried about wheeling the wrong way anymore. Rick picked up the baton, and out we marched. When we did the crossing pattern, I had to cross opposite Mike. He gave me a wink as he passed. My eyes smiled back, but my heart didn't beat wildly as it did when Brad smiled at me.

Then the team came out, and we escorted them down the field. Of course I couldn't help noticing Brad. As he passed me, he gave me his wonderful smile.

Soon Brad Sorensen will be just a memory, I thought. Someone to tell the girls about when I go to my new school. How I wished I had some special memories of him to take with me, not just occasional smiles and his arm around my shoulder to make Raven jealous. If only we would have a last tender scene.

I could see it all. The game was over, and we were sitting in the empty bleachers, the moonlight falling on us and lighting up Brad's smile as he looked at me. "I can't tell you how much I'll miss you, Lisa," he whispered. "But Los Angeles is not the end of the world. I'll drive down on weekends. Maybe I can change my scholarship to UCLA instead of Berkeley."

"Oh, Brad, don't change your plans just for me. Your career comes first."

"You always were understanding, Lisa," he whispered. "But I have to be with you. . . ." Then he kissed me, tenderly but hungrily, as if we both knew that that kiss had to last for a long, long time. . . .

"Hey, Lisa, wake up," Shannon hissed in my ear. She poked me in the ribs with her clarinet. The band was just about to start marching to its place in the bleachers. Shannon had just saved me from another embarrassing scene. Thank goodness.

Will I ever grow out of this daydreaming? I asked myself as I settled down next to Shannon and arranged my music. And then it hit me. Soon I'd be back with Mama again. Back where I wanted to be and everything would be fine and I'd never have to pretend anymore! Surely the dreaming would stop then.

With a crack of helmets and several agonized grunts, the game started. I had never been particularly enthusiastic about football. For one thing it is always so hard to see what's happening, particularly if you don't understand the game too well, which I don't. Every time I followed one guy, thinking he had the ball, the ball turned up somewhere completely different. Or the quarterback would pass, and I wouldn't be able to see who caught it. So I gave up on the game and let my eyes wander through the stands, over the black outline of the hills and finally to the moon, which hung like a large, ripe orange above the mist. It was the harvest moon, not silver and cold and faraway, but full and rich and heavy as it is only once a year.

Then suddenly my thoughts were brought

back to earth by the play on the field, which had moved close to us. There was a scuffle, and two players leaped for the ball and crashed to the ground together right in front of us. They were so close I actually felt the ground vibrate and heard their groans as they collided. They got to their feet slowly, one rubbing an injured knee, the other gingerly testing his shoulder. Two coaches ran across the field to check out their players. The injured knee was escorted away, hobbling painfully. The shoulder was pronounced OK, but told to rest awhile. Discouraged, he pulled off his helmet. Brad!

As the coach walked ahead of him down the sideline, his gaze strayed in my direction, and his eyes met mine for a moment. Then his face lit up with a smile as he leaned across the flute players to say something to me. "You want to come to a party tomorrow night?" he asked. "I'll pick you up at your house at eight, OK?"

"OK," I managed to say.

"Great," he said and ran off after his coach.

"*Now* I know why you look so sexy tonight," Shannon said knowingly. "Brad Sorensen." She exhaled out loud, looking impressed. "Not bad."

All I could do was grin stupidly. I was floating on a pink cloud. I almost needed to pinch myself to see if it was real or another of my famous daydreams. It happened just like I dreamed it would, I realized in wonder.

But a little, nagging worry crept onto my cloud. Had Mike heard what Brad said? More important, just *why* was Brad asking me? Had he and Raven broken up for good? Even in my current status as an outcast, I thought I'd have heard about something as earth-shattering as that. And if they hadn't broken up, then what was Brad pulling?

Oh, come on, I told myself firmly. Give yourself credit. Maybe he really likes you. You're a good kid. Anyway, this is what you've been hoping for for weeks. Enjoy it!

Then suddenly wheels started turning in my head. Mike! Saturday night!

"Oh, heck," I said out loud, making Shannon look at me in surprise.

"What's wrong?" she asked.

"Oh, I just thought of something awful," I said.

The awful thing, of course, was that I had promised Mike I'd go to the concert with him Saturday night.

Chapter Nineteen

It was Saturday morning, and I felt terrible. I had just come back from seeing Mike. I had spent the whole night trying to think up a good story to tell him so that I wouldn't hurt him. It had to be believable and heartwarming. I discarded the stories about my grandmother being sick, needing me to help her fix a special dinner, plan the church bazaar, pick the late tomatoes, etc. They were all too easy to check on. I thought about telling him the truth. "Mike," I would say, "for the past month or so I have dreamed of nothing but a date with Brad Sorensen. I can't pass this one up now. You understand, don't you?" But I knew that he wouldn't.

The next bunch of stories consisted of: 1. a planned phone call from my mother, due right in the middle of the concert; 2. a planned phone call from father, due at roughly the same time; 3. having to work late at the store; 4. falling off my bike and spraining my ankle.

None of them was good enough.

In the end I resorted to that old standby, the terrible headache. From allergies, so I could

149

reasonably suggest it might stick around for a while. Also nobody could prove I didn't have a headache, and if I did have a headache, the last place I would want to be was at a concert.

Mike was washing his father's car when I went over to his house.

"Just the person I need," he said as he caught sight of me. "Grab a sponge and you can help."

"No, thanks," I said. "I wouldn't trust you with that hose."

"Do I look untrustworthy?" he asked innocently. "Many people have said I look angelic. The typical Boy Scout."

"I wouldn't trust a Boy Scout either."

"How can you say a thing like that?"

"Actually, Mike, I came to tell you something. See, I'm not feeling much like washing cars or anything else," I said. What I was thinking was that it would probably be a lot of fun to have a water fight with Mike. It was a lot of fun to do most things with him.

"What's wrong?" he asked, his face so full of concern that I felt like a real heel.

"Nothing serious. I just have this terrible headache. It's allergies. I get them around this time of year, and they last for hours."

"Oh, that's too bad," he said. "You better go and take a couple of aspirins right now, so you can shake it off before the concert."

"That's what I came to see you about, Mike. The concert. I can't go. I know I won't get rid of this headache in time. Nothing makes them go unless I dose myself so heavily with antihistamines that I'm dopey for twenty-four hours. . . . I'm sorry, Mike."

"Yeah, I'm sorry, too," he said, looking down at the hose in his hand. "But I guess a headache is a headache."

He looked up and his eyes met mine.

He knows, I thought. He knows I'm faking. He knows I'm inventing an excuse not to go to the concert with him.

I wanted to explain. I wanted to let him know that only something as important as a date with Brad would make me lie to him. Instead, I said, "It was only a concert, Mike. There will be other evenings."

"Yeah, sure," he said, turning back to his soapy sponge and the car.

I walked away, feeling pretty bad. I knew other girls stood boys up and told white lies and changed boyfriends without blinking an eye and without a trace of guilt. I guess I just wasn't that sort of girl. Even the thought of a date with Brad in a few hours couldn't make me feel better.

The afternoon went by quickly and painlessly enough since I was working in the store. As usual, we were so busy I didn't have time to think about anything except the job. There wasn't even time for one teeny little daydream.

By the time I got home and had dinner, I only had a little over an hour to get ready. I had planned to soak in the tub and do the things I never did, like buff my nails and pluck my eyebrows. Instead, I had to bag that plan and settle for a quick shower to wash my hair. I knew from experience that washing and blow drying my hair would take over half an hour, and that didn't leave long for putting on clothes and makeup.

All I need now, I thought, is Mike dropping by to see how my headache is! That set off the worrying again. I worried about Mike leaving his house at the same time as me, even though I knew the concert was due to start at eight, which was when Brad was picking me up. But what if Mike left late? I wished I had arranged to meet Brad at the party. I wished I could go in disguise. After all, this was a small town, and it was quite likely that I would bump into someone who knew both Mike and me. Like Raven. I had hardly allowed myself time to think of her. What if she was at the party?

Why are you making such a big thing out of this anyway? I asked myself as I sat staring into the mirror holding the blow dryer. You are not married to Mike Gibson. You are not even going steady with him. And Brad is not married to Raven. You are both perfectly free to date whomever you want to.

So why did I still feel guilty? And scared?

I finished my hair and put on my silk dress, the one good thing I had brought with me from Hollywood. It was a deep blue with long sleeves and a low neckline, and it fitted me as if it had been handmade for me. I brushed out my hair and caught it back on one side with a barrette and then put on just enough makeup to make my cheeks glow and to make my eyes seem as blue as the dress. When I was through, I had to admit I had done a good job.

"Well, who would have thought it," I said to the gorgeous face in the mirror. "You look very pretty! Lana Daniels wouldn't recognize her own daughter if she saw her now."

The doorbell rang, and I bounded down the stairs two at a time in a most undignified and unfeminine way, reaching the door at the same time Grandma did. "You look lovely, dear," she said, and I gave her a quick hug before I opened the door. I think she suspected how important this date was to me.

Brad smiled when he saw me, a smile that said he liked the way I looked. I introduced Grandma and Brad, and after a brief chat Grandma disappeared. She's very understanding. Brad and I stepped into the chilly evening.

This will be an evening I'll remember all my life, I thought as we drove through the quiet streets in Brad's car.

Music was already spilling out from a white frame house as we pulled up beside the picket fence. The street was full of cars. We walked up the front path and through the open door. Inside the music was so loud the whole house was vibrating. The air was heavy with smoke.

A girl I knew slightly from school came over to us. "Hi, Brad, glad you could make it." She glanced at me curiously.

"This is Lisa," Brad said. "She's my date tonight."

The girl looked at me with surprise and interest. "What happened to Raven?" she whispered to Brad. It was not easy to be discreet under such circumstances.

"We had a disagreement," Brad said. "She made me choose between football and her. I chose football. Come on, Lisa." He took my hand and led me to the back room.

The room was already full of dancing kids. It had one of those psychedelic lights in a corner, flashing on and off and making the couples appear to be moving in slow motion one minute and fast motion the next. Smoke drifted upward and glimmered as the light caught it, making the scene seem more unreal than ever. If it hadn't been for Brad's strong hand supporting my arm, I would have thought I was in the middle of a dream.

"Come on, let's dance," he said, and we began moving with the rest of the kids. Then the music changed to a slow number. Brad's arms came around me and pulled me to him. My head nestled against his chest. His hands moved caressingly up and down my spine, bringing out goose bumps.

I've waited all my life for this, I thought in

amazement. It's actually happening. I am here, dancing with Brad Sorensen. His arms are around me. He is holding me tight. Then another thought crept into my mind. And I'll be going away and leaving him any day now. Going to live with my mother, and I'll never see him again.

Brad bent his head down to nuzzle and kiss my ear.

I won't go, I decided suddenly. I'm not going to give this up now. I'll tell her I don't want to live with her. I want to stay here with Brad. Then I told myself I wasn't going to worry anymore that night. That evening belonged to Brad and me, and nothing in the whole world was going to spoil it.

"Well, who have we here?" spoke a frosty voice behind me. "Look at the happy couple."

"Hi, Raven," Brad said, not releasing his hold on me. "I figured you'd show up."

Chapter Twenty

The music stopped, and Raven stood in the doorway looking cool and beautiful in a long black dress. She was wearing feathers in her hair and looked like a witch doctor or something. Her eyes glinted like a snake's.

"If I'd known you were going to be here, I'd never have come," she said.

"Raven, you knew darn well I'd be here," Brad said. "But you couldn't resist seeing who I'd bring."

On either side of us, couples moved back toward the walls as if they were clearing the room for a fight.

"Lisa Daniels?" Raven said, smirking. "Couldn't you do any better than that?"

"Lisa is a nice girl," Brad said, "which is more than I can say for you. She's not all burned out at sixteen, like some people I could mention."

"Oh, really," Raven said smoothly. "So I'm all burned out, am I? That never seemed to bother you before."

A few kids laughed uneasily. I stood in the middle of it all, trapped by Brad's strong arms, feeling flushed and miserable and wishing I could escape.

"Bug off, will you, Raven?" Brad said. "Leave us to dance in peace."

"It's a free country," Raven said. "I can stand where I want to. And I want to stand here where I can keep an eye on you."

"It's nice to know I still matter so much to you," Brad said, smiling smugly and giving me a little squeeze.

Raven's eyes flashed dangerously. "I thought all football players were dumb," she said, "so how come you're so full of wisecracks?"

"Some football players have it all," Brad said. "They're smart and cute and strong. But you don't want a football player, remember? You want someone who can spend one hundred per-cent of his time worshipping you."

"Shut up, Brad," Raven snapped. She turned sharply and left the room. The music started again. People shuffled back onto the floor. Brad held me close to him again, but it wasn't the same. Finally he let go of me and said, "I'll get us something to drink. Wait right here."

I waited. Another dance began, but he didn't come back. I began to feel embarrassed, leaning against the wall alone while other couples moved past me. Some of them glanced in my direction as they passed, and some whispered to each other.

At last I had had enough. I went out of the room to find Brad. He wasn't at the refreshment table. He wasn't in the hall. I opened the door to a room that was quite dark. Someone was in there, but it wasn't Brad. The voice that swore at me sounded quite different from his. He wasn't in the kitchen either. I went to the back door and opened it. It led to a small, dark square of lawn, bordered with flower beds. As I was about to step out, a boy grabbed my arm.

"Don't go out there," he said.

"Why not?"

"It would be better if you didn't," he said, trying to bring me back inside.

"Let go of me," I said, breaking away from him. I stepped down into the garden. As my eyes got used to the dark, I saw a couple kissing passionately on a bench in the corner. I saw the feathers in Raven's hair and Brad's chino pants. I turned away and walked back into the house.

The boy was looking at me kindly. "I think he wanted to make her jealous. It looks like it worked, too. Do you want me to give you a ride home?"

"No," I said, pushing past him. "Thanks. I'll be all right. I'll walk."

I pushed my way roughly down the hall and out of the house and down the street. I didn't stop running until I was several blocks away. Then I had to stop, panting, under a huge eucalyptus tree. Its sweet smell was all around me and calmed me a bit. My heart was hammering in my chest as I fought back the tears.

Why had I been so stupid? Why hadn't I seen through it earlier? Of course a popular guy like Brad wouldn't choose a girl like me. He only chose me because I meant something to Raven, because I was the one who could really make her mad. I had been part of a calculated plot to get them back together again. And now they were together, and I didn't matter at all.

I'm sure everyone will have a good laugh when they hear about it, I thought. I expect it will be all around school on Monday, and—and this time I can't expect Mike to protect me. Suddenly I wanted to see Mike. If only he were here, he would comfort me. He would know what to say to make me feel better. He would—

Then it hit me fully what I had done to Mike. I remembered his hurt face when he had said, "I suppose a headache is a headache." I had used him, and now I had been used. And it hurt. It hurt badly.

You deserve it, I told myself bitterly. This was all because of a stupid daydream about a boy who never existed. I've missed being with a boy who did exist and did care. Just because Mike didn't look like my Mr. Right, I never even gave him a chance. If only I could tell him how sorry I am, I thought. But I don't suppose he'd want to hear. But at least I can try.

I made a decision: I would wait for him to come out of the concert; I would make him listen; I'd tell him I was wrong. It isn't goose bumps that are important, I thought. It's having someone who cares about you all the time, who is there when you need him, who won't let you down.

I broke into a run again, listening to the echoes of my own footsteps. It sounded as if someone were running beside me. I cut down a dark, narrow street, pounding through an unfamiliar part of town.

I didn't stop running until I had crossed the square and was standing outside the town hall. It seemed so deserted that I panicked: the concert must have ended, and everyone had already gone home. But when I looked at my watch in the light of a streetlamp, I saw that it was only nine-thirty. I could hardly believe it. I checked the town hall clock, and it said nine-thirty, too. All that running for nothing! My evening had been so full of drama, it felt more like eleven to me. Anyway, the concert didn't end until after ten, so I had a nice long wait.

I found a bench near the bus stop where I had first arrived so long ago and shrank back into the shadows where no one could see me. A couple came past. He had his arm around her shoulders, and she was looking up into his face as he spoke.

That's what I've been missing, I thought. That could have been Mike and me if only I hadn't been so stupid.

Then a horrible thought came into my mind. What if Mike had taken someone else to the concert? After all, why should he go alone? I saw the picture clearly. . . . Mike and another girl coming down the steps holding hands and laughing. "I thought I was interested in Lisa Daniels for a while," he was saying, "but she wasn't interested in me. I'm glad she wasn't free for the concert tonight, or I'd never have had the chance to be with you." And they would walk right by without even noticing me.

At last the town hall clock chimed out ten, and about fifteen minutes later the concert ended. The big doors opened, and light spilled out. People came down the steps in little groups, chatting and smiling. I looked everywhere for Mike, but I didn't see him. Then another thought occurred to me: he didn't go at all because I wouldn't go with him. He gave his tickets to someone else and stayed home.

I got up from my seat in the shadows. The crowd was thinning out. Still no Mike. A man came out of the hall and started to close the doors. I heard the scrape of metal against stone as he dragged the doors shut.

"Is everyone out?" I asked him.

"Unless they're hiding," he said and pushed the door shut with a hollow clang.

I turned and walked away. That was the last straw. I began the long walk home. I started off slowly. I was wearing tight shoes, and they hurt me after all the running I'd done.

This is my punishment, I thought. I had this coming to me. But I couldn't help feeling sorry for myself, like a character in a fairy story turned out into a storm by a wicked stepmother.

I heard a car behind me. It slowed down until it was crawling along beside me. Now someone's going to try to pick me up, I thought. I don't think I can take much more tonight. If he says anything to me, I'm going to run to that house with the light on and bang on the door until they open up.

I walked along with my chin held high. The car crawled along beside me. I heard the window being rolled down.

"Lisa? Is that you?" a voice called.

I stopped, not quite believing the voice I heard. "Mike?" I asked, peering into the darkness of the car.

"Lisa, what are you doing out here?" he asked sharply. "Don't you know it's crazy to walk alone at this time of night? Get in right now."

I climbed in.

"Now," he said, "do you mind telling me why someone with a headache is going on a seven-mile hike in the middle of the night dressed like Lady Macbeth?"

I looked at his face, his good-natured grin, his warm eyes, and suddenly all the tears came flooding out. "Oh, Mike," I sobbed, "you won't want to know me anymore after you hear this."

I told him the whole story, every sordid detail. It was all mixed up and interrupted with sobs and nose blowings, but he got the general idea. He sat there patiently and didn't say a word until I finished. Almost finished, that is. He interrupted toward the end to say, "And you walked all that way to the town hall to meet me? You must be crazy. That was through the worst part of town."

"I figured, but I didn't care about that. I just had to see you and tell you."

"Tell me what?"

"That I was wrong. That it's you I want. Brad may have been cute, but underneath he was nothing."

"You mean I'm not cute?" Mike asked. But before I could answer, he was drawing me toward him and kissing me. I didn't struggle to get free. I just let it happen.

"Mike," I said breathlessly when the kiss had ended, "I don't think about you as my big brother anymore."

Much later we headed for home. Mike drove slowly, with one arm around me.

"What I don't understand," I said, "is how you got out of that concert. I waited and watched all the people come past."

"Never heard of a side exit?" he said, squeezing me close to him. "I had my car parked in back of the building, so naturally I went out that way."

Mike stopped the car in front of my grandmother's house. I gave him a quick kiss goodnight, then jumped out. I silently let myself in the front door and tiptoed down the hall. It was past midnight, but my grandmother was a very light sleeper. I crept up the stairs one by one. Halfway up, a stair creaked, and I froze before going on. At the top I was surprised to find light coming from under my grandmother's door. She had probably fallen asleep reading again. She did that sometimes. I tiptoed in to turn off her light.

But when I opened her door, I saw her sitting at her desk, writing busily. She was still fully dressed.

"Grandma, is anything wrong?" I asked, suddenly filled with worry.

She spun around, looking startled. "Oh, Lisa, you scared me. I was thinking so hard, I didn't hear you come in."

"I hope you weren't waiting up for me," I said.

"Oh, no. I had a few things that needed taking care of and a lot on my mind, so I didn't think there was much point in trying to go to sleep."

"Is anything wrong?" I asked again.

"No, not really," she answered, her face relaxing into a tired smile. "In fact, everything is fine. Just fine. And you should be the first to know—" She paused and played with her pen. "Herbie came over tonight. He's been trying to get me to marry him for years. I've always turned him down. I like my independence too much. But since you've been here, I've begun to know the companionship I've been missing all these years. I've gotten used to having someone around the house again. Someone to talk to and share things with. And, well, when Herbie brought up marriage again tonight, I thought, well, why not? You'll be going to college soon, and, after all, this place is getting a bit much for me to run alone. But Herbie and I together would manage fine. And since he doesn't mind moving in here, it's not like I'd have to give up much of anything. Besides, Herbie's a good man. We'll take care of each other. So I finally said yes!"

"That's wonderful, Grandma!" I cried. "I'm so happy for you!"

So Herbie would move in with Grandma. That was a surprise.

She smiled at me. "He was funny, Lisa. I wish you could have seen him. When I said yes, Herbie jumped up and said, 'Edith, you've made me the happiest man in Sonoma County.' Then he went home. He said it wasn't good for my reputation if he stayed after ten!"

We both laughed.

"I'm glad you'll have someone to look after you, Grandma," I said. "I hope I'm here to be a bridesmaid."

"I hope so, too," she said.

I gave her a kiss. Grandma smiled and looked at me for a long time. "Good night," she said at last. "You ought to get some sleep now. We'll talk more in the morning."

"OK," I said. "You get some sleep, too, Grandma."

"I will. I was just going through papers, but that can wait."

I walked to the door.

"Oh, I clean forgot to ask," she called after me. "How did your evening go?"

My face broke into a silly grin. "Just as I always hoped an evening would," I said.

Then I went back to my own room. Well, that's that, Lisa Daniels, I thought. Your fate is sealed.

Until that moment part of me had secretly hoped Mama would change her mind and I could stay on here. Especially now that I had Mike. But when Grandma married Herbie, would she still want me? She and Herbie would be busy building their new life together. Would I fit in it? I wasn't positive there was a place for me here anymore. It was a disturbing thought, and I fell asleep to uneasy dreams.

But the next few days were the sweetest I had ever known. With Mike beside me, every little event turned into something unforgettable and fun. I tried not to let myself think about the past or the future. It would have been too easy to regret that I could have had happiness earlier or that it was only going to last a little while longer. But I was firm with myself. No more daydreams and no more looking back or forward, wishing for what might have been or might possibly be. Just today.

And today was great! One Sunday I went with Mike and his family to help pick grapes at his uncle's vineyard. I had never realized hard manual work could also be fun if you were doing it with the right person. We all worked in a long line, laughing and teasing each other. Sometimes Mike would catch me off-guard with a well-directed grape, and sometimes I would return the compliment. At the end of the day we all got together in the winery yard, surrounded by box after box of dark purple grapes.

"It's a shame they have to be so hygienic these days," Mike said. "I'd rather stamp on them barefoot in those big wooden vats."

"Yech," I said. "If I thought your toenails had been in my wine, I'd never drink it!"

Mike laughed. "Come on. Let's go try some."

"Mike, I don't drink," I protested.

"Oh, well, actually neither do I, but I want to show you something anyway. Come on." He led me down the path.

"Where are you taking me?" I asked. We were walking away from the house into dense undergrowth, and the steep side of the hill loomed up before us.

"Aha!" he cried. "I guess you might as well know. You see, I am not a simple high-school boy at all but Count Frankenfurter, and I'm taking you to my dungeon laboratory where you will be transformed into a large canned ham, eaten by consumers, and never heard from again." He said all this with an unidentifiable European accent.

He pushed aside the undergrowth, and there

was a door in the hillside. It was half-open. "In you go, my pretty one," he cackled. "You vill never escape—never." He dragged me inside. Even though I knew it was just Mike fooling around, my skin prickled as I went through that door.

Then I had a big surprise. Inside was a large cave, cool and dry and cozy. Huge barrels, towering right up to the ceiling, lined the walls, and near the entrance were tables and chairs. The tables were covered with checkered cloths and were lit by candles. On them were arranged huge trays of food and bottles of wine.

"We always have a feast at the end of the picking," Mike said. "It's a family tradition."

I think that was the very best evening I ever remembered. We sat in the flickering candlelight in the midst of a happy group, laughing at the stupid jokes. It was something I had never experienced. My parents had given parties, and lots of boring people came, all elegantly dressed. They drank too much and talked about themselves all evening. I had never been to a real family party before. Mike's family was a large one, and each person was just as bad about teasing as Mike himself.

Mike's aunt was a huge woman who thought everybody was about to die of starvation and kept pressing more food on us even when we were too stuffed to speak. Then someone got out a guitar and began to sing. Everyone joined in the chorus and clanked their forks against the glasses in accompaniment. The guitar was passed around, and one cousin after another played and sang, sometimes sad songs, sometimes lively ones, sometimes funny ones.

I beamed as I looked around at the group, knowing I was not an outsider watching it but a real part of it—Mike's girl, someone who belonged.

"Did you have a good time?" Mike asked as we drove home crowded into his parents' car.

"Good? It was wonderful. You don't know how lucky you are to have a family like that, a real, old-fashioned family, and a place where you really belong."

Mike slipped his arm around me. I knew he understood.

Chapter Twenty-One

"You're not really going trick-or-treating, are you?" my grandmother asked in disbelief. "Kids *your* age?"

October had gone by with no word from my mother. Sometimes I almost managed to forget she was coming for me. Grandma understood my hurt and was comforting. She never said, "I told you so."

I started to remember a few of the less pleasant aspects of living with my mother. I remembered how she'd sulk when things didn't go her way. I remembered how she tried to organize my life for me, choose my friends and my clothes. And most of all, I remembered she had left me without saying goodbye.

But now there was no choice. Grandmother was bustling around getting ready for Herbie. He had put his own house up for sale and kept lugging loads of stuff over to Grandma's.

If it hadn't been for Mike, I might have cracked up. But he was there with me every day, making me laugh, loving me, saying things that made me feel better.

"We wouldn't have to be apart," he said.

"We only have one more year of school. Maybe we could go to the same college. Maybe your mother will give you your own car, and you could drive up to visit over vacations. Maybe it won't ever happen."

"Sure," I said, unconvinced.

He smiled and touched my hair. "It will all work out. Things have a way of turning out right."

"How can you be such an optimist all the time," I said in a whine.

He got to his feet. "I can see stronger therapy is needed to shake you out of your state of depression," he said. "Come on, let's go pick our Halloween costumes."

"We can't go out trick-or-treating. We're too old."

"There's no age limit!" he informed me. "Besides, who'll recognize us? We might be tall third-graders!"

So we spent an afternoon up in Mike's attic trying on old clothes. Mike wanted to go in his mother's old prom dress, but I refused to be seen with him looking like that. In the end we settled on going as a couple of tramps in old farm overalls, battered straw hats, and huge hobnailed boots. We giggled as we made up each other's faces, giving ourselves red noses and bushy eyebrows, and blacking out our front teeth.

My grandmother shook her head as we

clomped out of the house that night, clutching our empty bags.

"Don't blame me," she called after us, "if they lock you up and take you straight to the padded cell in the state mental hospital."

But we didn't care. It was a perfect Halloween night, cold and crisp with a big, golden October moon hanging just above the horizon. The smell of wood smoke was in the air, and leaves crackled underfoot. The street was a well of darkness sheltering strange shadows—those of ghosts and monsters and witches, giggling as they ran. At one house we arrived at the door just behind a group of tiny monsters and a tinier princess. They rang the bell, and the door was opened by a man dressed as an executioner carrying a hangman's noose from which a dead chicken dangled. The tiny kids gave one look at him, then turned and ran screaming down the path without waiting for their candy. But we, being made of sterner stuff, stayed on and opened our sacks.

"Ain't you guys kind of big to be out getting candy?" the executioner growled.

"Not me, sir," Mike said in a tiny voice. "I'm just standing on my brother's shoulders."

We took the candy and ran.

At last we turned back onto our own street.

"Thank goodness," I said. "My feet are killing me. I was never meant to wear boots like you country bumpkins."

"City-bred weaklings ain't got no stamina,"

Mike said in his best hillbilly voice. "We country folks jest keep on a-walking until our feet fall off—which might happen to me any minute now," he added in an undertone.

A car came slowly down the street and pulled up behind us. A large, balding man poked his head out of the window.

"Hey, you over there," he called to us.

"You want me, sir?" Mike called back, still using his hillbilly voice.

"Yeah. Can you come here a minute?" the man asked.

Mike shuffled over like a bewildered country bumpkin.

"You want to talk to *me*, sir?" he asked, scratching his head.

"Yes," the man snapped. "Are we on the right street for Mrs. Daniels's house? We've been driving around for hours and can't find the thing."

"Mrs. Daniels's house?" Mike repeated. He stopped and scratched his head again. "Can't say I've ever heard of a Daniels's house. You ever hear of a Daniels's house, Lullabelle?" he called across to me.

"Can't say that I have," I answered seriously.

The man muttered something like "idiots," revved up the car savagely, and drove on. We collapsed in helpless laughter.

"Well, he shouldn't have been so rude," Mike said as we walked home. "Treating us as if we were peasants or something. He deserved everything he got."

"I wonder who they were," I said thoughtfully. "Why would they want my grandmother at this time of night?"

"We'll find out in a few minutes."

We reached our driveway.

"Well, it looks like they found the house anyway," Mike said. The white car was parked in our driveway.

"We better sneak in through the back door," I said. "We don't want them to see us."

We tiptoed through the kitchen and halfway up the stairs. Voices came from the living room. Then that same darn stair creaked again.

"Is that you, Lisa?" my grandmother called. The living room door opened, and her head poked out. "Come on down and meet my visitors." She looked a little grim.

"But, Grandma, I can't go in there looking like this," I pleaded.

"That doesn't matter," she said with a mischievous smile. "They'd just love to see how you look."

"This is where I disappear," Mike hissed in my ear. "Call me when they've gone."

"Coward," I hissed back.

"You bet," he said and left.

I came downstairs slowly and, feeling very foolish, entered the sitting room. The man with he bald head looked up and scowled. The woman beside him leaped to her feet.

"Lisa," she called. "My baby!"

Chapter Twenty-Two

"Mama?" I asked hesitantly. I hardly recognized her. She seemed older than I remembered, and her face was harder. Still beautiful, but tougher and older behind its shell of makeup.

"Lisa," she said, throwing her arms open wide, "come and give me a big hug. Let me see how much you've grown."

But I hung back self-consciously. "Let me go up and change first, Mama. Then you'll see what I look like."

"What were you doing, rehearsing for a play?" she asked, giving a high little laugh.

"No, it's Halloween. We were out trick-or treating."

"A little old for that," the man muttered, making me aware of him for the first time.

"Oh, don't be such an old stick-in-the-mud," my mother said, grabbing his arm. "Lisa, darling, this is my dearest Mort. I want you two to like each other."

"I'll go up and change first," I said.

"Is this going to take long?" the man asked. "We've got that long drive back to San Fran

176

cisco tonight, and you know how I hate driving in the dark."

"Try and be quick, won't you, honey?" my mother pleaded.

I fled. So that was my new stepfather—that fat, bald, scowling man who clearly didn't like me. Did I really have to go home with him? I knew there was no way I could ever call him Daddy.

Upstairs I made like a quick-change artist. Then I brushed out my hair and went slowly downstairs.

"Well, don't you look nice," my mother said approvingly. "See, Mort, I told you she looked like me."

"Mm-hmm," he said expansively, his face creasing into what might have been an attempt at a smile. "Well, kid, what are you going to do with your life?" he asked in a supreme effort to make conversation.

"I'll decide that when I manage to get through being a teenager," I said. I hadn't meant it to sound rude, but somehow it came out that way.

Mort's face slipped back into its scowl. "What you need is a good school," he said. "Lots of work, lots of discipline. Young people have to be molded. That's what all teenagers need to learn these days—discipline and respect. You don't learn stuff like that in any old school."

I shot my mother a pleading glance. To be living in the same house as Mort would be bad enough, but to go to the sort of school he had in mind . . . Surely she would be on my side. Apparently she was, because she patted his arm and said, "Now, Mort, we've been through all that."

"Yeah," he growled. "Your mother's too soft-hearted. She doesn't want to send you to boarding school."

"So what school will I be going to?" I asked. "Will I go back to Hollywood High? Where are we going to be living?"

There was a moment's hesitation before my mother said, "Well, it's like this, Lisa. I mean that's what we came up here to tell you. You see, I told you Mort was my agent. Well, it turns out he's an absolute *miracle* worker. He knows *everybody* in the business, and he's got this marvelous part for me in a wonderful new film."

"That's great, Mama," I said because there was this pause, and I felt it was expected of me.

"So I wanted to pop up here and make sure you were all right before we leave."

"Leave?" I was feeling confused. "Am I—mean, I thought I was going to live with you."

My mother toyed with her ruby ring. "Well, that's just it, baby. That's what I've been trying to say. We leave for Europe next week. I'm going to be shooting in Spain all winter, and then well, what it comes down to is there won't be a home for you with me. Not for awhile, anyway. You do understand, don't you?"

A feeling of tremendous relief swept over

me. I wouldn't have to see Mort again! At the same time I remembered Grandma was getting married.

"But what's going to happen to me?" I blurted out. "Grandma's getting—"

"Getting very excited you'll be living with me," Grandma said firmly. "Are you folks sure I can't fix you something to eat before you head back?"

Mort got to his feet. "No, thank you. We have a six o'clock flight to take out of San Francisco in the morning, so we should be leaving now. Come on, Lana, say goodbye and let's get going."

"Goodbye, baby," my mother said, giving me a hug and overpowering me with her perfume.

"Goodbye, Mama."

"Take care of yourself."

"Don't worry about me. I'm fine," I said.

Mort got up and walked to the front door. I couldn't resist a parting shot. "Goodbye, Daddy," I called.

I saw the back of his neck go bright pink. They walked out.

Grandma and I were left alone in the sitting room.

"What's going to happen now?" I asked frantically. "I can't let you ruin your life because of me."

My grandmother smiled. "Silly girl. Ruin my life! Honey, you've made it a hundred times

more interesting! If you only knew the argu
ments I'd had about you with Herbie."

"About me?"

"Yes. Herbie's wanted you to stay with us
all along. 'She's such a nice girl. I'm so fond o.
her,' he kept saying. 'I don't like the thought o1
her running around in Hollywood. We can give
her a much better home here.' He said he'd
always wanted a daughter of his own."

"Herbie actually wants me?" I asked. This
was new—people fighting over me for a change!

"And you, Grandma?" I asked doubtfully.
"You said you argued with Herbie. You didn'
want me here."

"It wasn't what I wanted, honey," she said.
"It was what you wanted. And I thought you
really wanted to be with your mother again,
although I had my doubts about her convic-
tions. So I was willing to let you go—until I saw
that awful man. Then I knew there was no way
I was going to let you go. I was going to fight in
any way I knew how to keep you here."

"Oh, Grandma," I said, "I love you." And I
flung my arms around her.

We sat there for awhile in silence, rocking
each other. Then my grandmother became her
old self again and straightened up. "Well, I think
I ought to phone Herbie and tell him the good
news," she said. I caught her wiping her eyes
as she went. Suddenly she looked around. "And
what happened to Mike? I heard his voice when
you came in, didn't I?"

"He was a coward and ran home. We had just met my dear stepfather in the street." Then I told her about the joke we had played, and we both had a good laugh.

"Well, go on over and bring Mike back here," Grandma said after she had wiped her eyes, this time from laughing. "I made a nice big pot of soup for you two to have when you got back home."

"OK, great!" I said. "Boy, he won't believe it when he hears the news!" I ran toward the door.

Then Grandma called me back again. "Oh, Lisa, forget about the soup. We're going to have a real party! And I'm going to tell Herbie to come over, too. We've got something to celebrate!"

Chapter Twenty-Three

The sweet music floated across the hall. In front of me couples were dancing, the skirts of the girls' dresses swaying like a field of flowers.

I stood alone at the edge of the crowd and waited. Across the crowd I caught sight of a young man. His sandy hair was tamed into neat waves, and he looked strangely distinguished in a tuxedo, old and young at the same time. Through the twirling couples our eyes met. His eyes lit up, and he made his way over to me, carefully balancing two drinks.

Suddenly I remembered that evening long ago, when I had seen my dream man across the crowded party room, and he had smiled at me just like that. Only that Mr. Right hadn't fought his way across to me. This one did. Because this one was real, not just a daydream. I had said goodbye to daydreams forever. I didn't need them anymore.

"I thought I'd lost you," he said, putting down the drinks on a small table. "I hope you appreciate that I risked life and death to carry the drinks across that floor to you."

"I do appreciate it," I said, giving his hand a squeeze.

After we finished our drinks, he said, "Come on, let's dance." He took my hand and dragged me onto the floor. As we walked past other couples, I was conscious of the turned heads and the whispered comments.

But I didn't mind them anymore. The whispers were not saying, "That's Lana Daniels's daughter." They were saying, "That's Lisa with Mike. They're going together now."

It was the homecoming dance. That grand affair I thought I was going to miss. But I was there, in a new dress that looked as if it cost a hundred dollars—but didn't, thanks to a clever grandmother who made it, with a little help from me! I was wearing a corsage of peach-colored chrysanthemums. They were from Mike, of course, who looked incredibly handsome in his dark blue tuxedo.

And everything was just perfect. At last I was who I wanted to be and where I wanted to be. I was not Lana Daniels's daughter, but me, Lisa. I had stopped pretending forever. I didn't want to be like my mother anymore. It didn't worry me that she was beautiful and I would never be, that she was famous and I would probably never be that, either. That last visit had squashed my fantasy mother once and for all. I had seen an aging woman, who had nothing but her looks, fighting to stay young and successful, fighting any way she knew how, even if it meant taking up with a scowling, bald-headed bully. I felt sorry for her now. She had had a tough life, she was probably going to have a still tougher life, and I said a silent prayer of thanks that I was out of it. Instead of the glamour of Hollywood, I had funny old Herbie with his cracked voice and my loving grandmother and the chickens and tomatoes—and it was wonderful. Also I had Mike, which was more wonderful still!

We drifted across the dance floor, Mike holding me very close, our feet barely moving in time to the beat.

Another couple came up beside us and bumped into us as they passed.

"Well, if it isn't Lisa Daniels," Raven said. "So you got stuck with Mike Gibson after all, eh?"

Brad said nothing and looked slightly embarrassed.

I flashed her a stunning smile. "Nice seeing you, too, Alice," I said sweetly.

Raven's mouth dropped open about a foot. "Lisa!"

I figured some of Raven's friends knew her real name but that they wouldn't have dared to use it. Raven looked like a queen who had just been reprimanded by a serf. She tried to dance close enough to us to insult me back, but Mike, grinning evilly, whirled me away in his arms.

He whirled me right out onto the courtyard behind the gym. Lanterns were hanging in the trees, twinkling over the heads of a few couples who, like Mike and me, wanted some quiet and privacy. The air was chilly, and Mike took off his jacket and wrapped me in it. He led me to a stone bench, and we sat down. I laid my head on his shoulder, feeling dreamy and relaxed. Suddenly I realized something odd—I wasn't dreaming. I was enjoying. Mike's arms were around me, his lips brushing my forehead.

Hey, I thought, who needs daydreams? The real thing's a lot better!

I snuggled deeper into his arms, thinking of Grandma and Herbie and Jellybean. And Mike. All the things I loved. I had them now. I didn't need to dream anymore.

"Mike?" I whispered. "I'm not dreaming, am I?"

"I don't think so," he said. "Not unless I am, too."

I smiled at him. "Good," I said. "But if I were dreaming, this would be the best dream ever."